PENGUIN BOOKS

Casino Royale

Bond was not amused. 'What the hell do they want to send me a woman for?' he said bitterly. 'Do they think this is a bloody picnic?'

Mathis interrupted. 'Calm yourself, my dear James. She is as serious as you could wish and as cold as an icicle. She speaks French like a native and knows her job backwards. Her cover's perfect and I have arranged for her to team up with you quite smoothly. What is more natural than that you should pick up a pretty girl here? As a Jamaican millionaire,' he coughed respectfully, 'what with your hot blood and all, you would look naked without one.'

Bond grunted dubiously.

'Any other surprises?' he asked suspiciously.

D1014159

Ian Fleming was born in 1908 and educated at Eton. After a brief period at the Royal Military Academy at Sandhurst he went abroad to further his education. In 1931, having failed to get an appointment in the Foreign Office, he joined Reuters News Agency. During the Second World War he was Personal Assistant to the Director of Naval Intelligence at the Admiralty, rising to the rank of Commander. His wartime experiences provided him with a first-hand knowledge of secret operations.

After the war he became Foreign Manager of Kemsley Newspapers. He built his house, Goldeneye, in Jamaica and there at the age of forty-four he wrote *Casino Royale*, the first of the novels featuring Commander James Bond. By the time of his death in 1964, the James Bond adventures had sold more than forty million copies. *Dr No*, the first film featuring James Bond and starring Sean Connery, was released in 1962 and the Bond films continue to be huge international successes. He is also the author of the magical children's book *Chitty Chitty Bang Bang*.

The novels of Ian Fleming were immediately recognized as classic thrillers by his contemporaries Kingsley Amis, Raymond Chandler and John Betjeman. With the invention of James Bond, Ian Fleming created the greatest British fictional icon of the late twentieth century.

Casino Royale

IAN FLEMING

PENGUIN BOOKS

PENGUIN BOOKS

Published by the Penguin Group
Penguin Books Ltd, 80 Strand, London WC2R 0RL, England
Penguin Putnam Inc., 375 Hudson Street, New York, New York 10014, USA
Penguin Books Australia Ltd, 250 Camberwell Road, Camberwell,
Victoria 3124, Australia
Penguin Books Canada Ltd, 10 Alcorn Avenue, Toronto, Ontario, Canada M4V 3B2
Penguin Books India (P) Ltd, 11 Community Centre,
Panchsheel Park, New Delhi – 110 017, India
Penguin Books (NZ) Ltd, Cnr Rosedale and Airborne Roads,
Albany, Auckland, New Zealand
Penguin Books (South Africa) (Pty) Ltd, 24 Sturdee Avenue,
Rosebank 2196, South Africa

Penguin Books Ltd, Registered Offices: 80 Strand, London WC2R 0RL, England

www.penguin.com

First published by Jonathan Cape Ltd 1953
Published by Hodder and Stoughton 1988
Published simultaneously by Penguin and Viking 2002
10

Copyright © Glidrose Productions Ltd, 1953
All rights reserved

The moral right of the copyright holder has been asserted

Set in 9.75/14pt Melior
Typeset by Intype London Ltd
Printed in England by Clays Ltd, St Ives plc

CONTENTS

1 / THE SECRET AGENT

The scent and smoke and sweat of a casino are nauseating at three in the morning. Then the soul-erosion produced by high gambling – a compost of greed and fear and nervous tension – becomes unbearable and the senses awake and revolt from it.

James Bond suddenly knew that he was tired. He always knew when his body or his mind had had enough and he always acted on the knowledge. This helped him to avoid staleness and the sensual bluntness that breeds mistakes.

He shifted himself unobtrusively away from the roulette he had been playing and went to stand for a moment at the brass rail which surrounded breast-high the top table in the *salle privée*.

Le Chiffre was still playing and still, apparently, winning. There was an untidy pile of flecked hundred-mille plaques in front of him. In the shadow of his thick left arm there nestled a discreet stack of the big yellow ones worth half a million francs each.

Bond watched the curious, impressive profile for a time, and then he shrugged his shoulders to lighten his thoughts and moved away.

The barrier surrounding the *caisse* comes as high as

your chin and the *caissier*, who is generally nothing more than a minor bank clerk, sits on a stool and dips into his piles of notes and plaques. These are ranged on shelves. They are on a level, behind the protecting barrier, with your groin. The *caissier* has a cosh and a gun to protect him, and to heave over the barrier and steal some notes and then vault back and get out of the casino through the passages and doors would be impossible. And the *caissiers* generally work in pairs.

Bond reflected on the problem as he collected the sheaf of hundred thousand and then the sheaves of ten thousand franc notes. With another part of his mind, he had a vision of tomorrow's regular morning meeting of the casino committee.

'Monsieur Le Chiffre made two million. He played his usual game. Miss Fairchild made a million in an hour and then left. She executed three "bancos" of Monsieur Le Chiffre within an hour and then left. She played with coolness. Monsieur le Vicomte de Villorin made one million two at roulette. He was playing the maximum on the first and last dozens. He was lucky. Then the Englishman, Mister Bond, increased his winnings to exactly three million over the two days. He was playing a progressive system on red at table five. Duclos, the *chef de partie*, has the details. It seems that he is persevering and plays in maximums. He has luck. His nerves seem good. On the *soirée*, the chemin-defer won x, the baccarat won y and the roulette won z.

The boule, which was again badly frequented, still makes its expenses.'

'*Merci, Monsieur Xavier.*'

'*Merci, Monsieur le Président.*'

Or something like that, thought Bond as he pushed his way through the swing doors of the *salle privée* and nodded to the bored man in evening clothes whose job it is to bar your entry and your exit with the electric foot-switch which can lock the doors at any hint of trouble.

And the casino committee would balance its books and break up to its homes or cafés for lunch.

As for robbing the *caisse*, in which Bond himself was not personally concerned, but only interested, he reflected that it would take ten good men, that they would certainly have to kill one or two employees, and that anyway you probably couldn't find ten non-squeal killers in France, or in any other country for the matter of that.

As he gave a thousand francs to the *vestiaire* and walked down the steps of the casino, Bond made up his mind that Le Chiffre would in no circumstances try to rob the *caisse* and he put the contingency out of his mind. Instead he explored his present physical sensations. He felt the dry, uncomfortable gravel under his evening shoes, the bad, harsh taste in his mouth and the slight sweat under his arms. He could feel his eyes filling their sockets. The front of his face, his nose and antrum, were congested. He breathed the sweet night air deeply and focused his senses and his wits. He wanted to know if anyone had searched his room since he had left it before dinner.

He walked across the broad boulevard and through the gardens to the Hôtel Splendide. He smiled at the *concierge* who gave him his key – No. 45 on the first floor – and took the cable.

It was from Jamaica and read:

KINGSTONJA XXXX XXXXXX XXXX XXX
BOND SPLENDIDE ROYALE-LES-EAUX SEINE
INFERIEURE HAVANA CIGAR PRODUCTION ALL
CUBAN FACTORIES 1915 TEN MILLION REPEAT TEN
MILLION STOP HOPE THIS FIGURE YOU REQUIRE
REGARDS.

DASILVA

This meant that ten million francs was on the way to him. It was the reply to a request Bond had sent that afternoon through Paris to his headquarters in London asking for more funds. Paris had spoken to London where Clements, the head of Bond's department, had spoken to M, who had smiled wryly and told 'The Broker' to fix it with the Treasury.

Bond had once worked in Jamaica and his cover on the Royale assignment was that of a very rich client of Messrs Caffery, the principal import and export firm of Jamaica. So he was being controlled through Jamaica, through a taciturn man who was head of the picture desk on the *Daily Gleaner*, the famous newspaper of the Caribbean.

This man on the *Gleaner*, whose name was Fawcett, had been book-keeper for one of the leading turtle-fisheries on the Cayman Islands. One of the men from the Caymans who had volunteered on the outbreak of war, he had ended up as a Paymaster's clerk in a small Naval Intelligence organization in Malta. At the end of the war, when, with a heavy heart, he was due to return to the Caymans, he was spotted by the section of the Secret Service concerned with the Caribbean. He was strenuously trained in photography and in some other arts and, with the quiet connivance of an influential man in Jamaica, found his way to the picture desk of the *Gleaner*.

In the intervals between sifting photographs submitted by the great agencies – Keystone, Wide-World, Universal, INP, and Reuter-Photo – he would get peremptory instructions by telephone from a man he had never met to carry out certain simple operations requiring nothing but absolute discretion, speed, and accuracy. For these occasional services he received twenty pounds a month paid into his account with the Royal Bank of Canada by a fictitious relative in England.

Fawcett's present assignment was to relay immediately to Bond, full rates, the text of messages which he received at home by telephone from his anonymous contact. He had been told by this contact that nothing he would be asked to send would arouse the suspicion of the Jamaican post office. So he was not surprised to find himself suddenly appointed string correspondent for the 'Maritime Press and Photo Agency', with press-collect facilities to France and England, on a further monthly retainer of ten pounds.

He felt secure and encouraged, had visions of a BEM and made the first payment on a Morris Minor. He also bought a green eye-shade which he had long coveted and which helped him to impose his personality on the picture desk.

Some of this background to his cable passed through Bond's mind. He was used to oblique control and rather liked it. He felt it feather-bedded him a little, allowed him to give or take an hour or two in his communications with M. He knew that this was probably a fallacy, that probably there was another member of the Service at Royale-les-Eaux who was reporting independently, but it did give the illusion that he wasn't only 150 miles across the Channel from that deadly office building near Regent's Park, being watched and judged by those few cold brains that made the whole show work. Just as Fawcett, the Cayman Islander in Kingston, knew that if he bought that Morris Minor outright instead of signing the hire-purchase agreement, someone in London would probably know and want to know where the money had come from.

Bond read the cable twice. He tore a telegram form off the pad on the desk (why give them carbon copies?) and wrote his reply in capital letters:

He handed this to the *concierge* and put the cable signed 'Dasilva' in his pocket. The employers (if any) of the *concierge* could bribe a copy out of the local post office, if the *concierge* hadn't already steamed the envelope open or read the cable upside down in Bond's hands.

He took his key and said good night and turned to the stairs, shaking his head at the liftman. Bond knew what an obliging danger-signal a lift could be. He didn't expect anyone to be moving on the first floor, but he preferred to be prudent.

Walking quietly up on the balls of his feet, he regretted the *hubris* of his reply to M *via* Jamaica. As a gambler he knew it was a mistake to rely on too small a capital. Anyway, M probably wouldn't let him have any more. He shrugged his shoulders and turned off the stairs into the corridor and walked softly to the door of his room.

Bond knew exactly where the switch was and it was with one flow of motion that he stood on the threshold with the door full open, the light on and a gun in his hand. The safe, empty room sneered at him. He ignored the half-open door of the bathroom and, locking himself in, he turned up the bed-light and the mirror-light and threw his gun on the settee beside the window. Then he bent down and inspected one of his own black hairs which still lay undisturbed where he had left it before dinner, wedged into the drawer of the writing-desk.

Next he examined a faint trace of talcum powder on the inner rim of the porcelain handle of the clothes cupboard. It appeared immaculate. He went into the bathroom, lifted the cover of the lavatory cistern and verified the level of the water against a small scratch on the copper ball-cock.

Doing all this, inspecting these minute burglar-alarms, did not make him feel foolish or self-conscious. He was a secret agent, and still alive thanks to his exact attention to the detail of his profession. Routine precautions were to him no more unreasonable than they would be to a deep-sea diver or a test pilot, or to any man earning danger-money.

Satisfied that his room had not been searched while he was at the casino, Bond undressed and took a cold shower. Then he lit his seventieth cigarette of the day and sat down at the writing-table with the thick wad of his stake money and winnings beside him and entered some figures in a small note-book. Over the two days' play, he was up exactly three million francs. In London he had been issued with ten million, and he had asked London for a further ten. With this on its way to the local branch of Crédit Lyonnais, his working capital amounted to twenty-three million francs, or some twenty-three thousand pounds.

For a few moments Bond sat motionless, gazing out of the window across the dark sea, then he shoved the bundle of banknotes under the pillow of the ornate single bed, cleaned his teeth, turned out the lights and climbed with relief between the harsh French sheets. For ten minutes he lay on his left side reflecting on the events of the day. Then he turned over and focused his mind towards the tunnel of sleep.

His last action was to slip his right hand under the pillow until it rested under the butt of the .38 Colt Police Positive with the sawn barrel. Then he slept, and with the warmth and humour of his eyes extinguished, his features relapsed into a taciturn mask, ironical, brutal, and cold.

Two weeks before, this memorandum had gone from Station S of the Secret Service to M, who was then and is today head of this adjunct to the British Defence Ministries:

To: M.

From: Head of S.

Subject: A project for the destruction of Monsieur Le Chiffre (alias 'The Number', 'Herr Nummer', 'Herr Ziffer', etc.), one of the Opposition's chief agents in France and undercover Paymaster of the 'Syndicat des Ouvriers d'Alsace', the Communist-controlled trade union in the heavy and transport industries of Alsace, and as we know, an important fifth column in the event of war with Redland.

Documentation: Head of Archives' biography of Le Chiffre is attached at *Appendix A*. Also, *Appendix B*, a note on SMERSH.

We have been feeling for some time that Le Chiffre is getting into deep water. In nearly all respects he is an admirable agent of the USSR, but his gross physical habits and predilections are an Achilles heel of which we have been able to take advantage from time to time and one of his mistresses is a Eurasian (No. 1860) controlled by Station F, who has recently been able to obtain insight into his private affairs.

Briefly, it seems that Le Chiffre is on the brink of a financial crisis. Certain straws in the wind were noticed by 1860 – some discreet sales of jewellery, the disposal of a villa at Antibes, and a general tendency to check the loose spending which has always been a feature of his way of life. Further inquiries were made with the help of our friends of the Deuxième Bureau (with whom we have been working jointly on this case) and a curious story has come to light.

In January 1946, Le Chiffre bought control of a chain of brothels, known as the Cordon Jaune, operating in Normandy and Brittany. He was foolish enough to employ for this purpose some fifty million francs of the moneys entrusted to him by Leningrad Section III for the financing of SODA, the trade union mentioned above.

Normally the Cordon Jaune would have proved a most excellent investment and it is possible that Le Chiffre was motivated more by a desire to increase his union funds than by the hope of lining his own pocket by speculating with his employers' money. However that may be, it is clear that he could have found many investments more savoury than prostitution, if he had not been tempted by the by-product of unlimited women for his personal use.

Fate rebuked him with terrifying swiftness.

Barely three months later, on 13 April, there was passed in France Law No. 46685 entitled *Loi Tendant à la Fermeture des Maisons de Tolérance et au Renforcement de la Lutte contre le Proxénitisme*.

(When M came to this sentence he grunted and pressed a switch on the intercom.

'Head of S?'

'Sir.'

'What the hell does this word mean?' He spelt it out.

'Pimping, sir.'

'This is not the Berlitz School of Languages, Head of S. If you want to show off your knowledge of foreign jaw-breakers, be good enough to provide a crib. Better still, write in English.'

'Sorry, sir.'

M released the switch and turned back to the memorandum.

This law [he read] known popularly as 'La Loi Marthe Richard', closing all houses of ill-fame and forbidding the sale of pornographic books and films, knocked the bottom out of his investment almost overnight and suddenly Le Chiffre was faced with a serious deficit in his union funds. In desperation he turned his open houses into *maisons de passe*, where clandestine rendezvous could be arranged on the border-line of the law, and he continued to operate one or two *cinémas bleus* underground, but these shifts in no way served to cover his overheads, and all attempts to sell his investment, even at a heavy loss, failed dismally. Meanwhile the Police des Moeurs were on his trail and in a short while twenty or more of his establishments were closed down.

The police were, of course, only interested in this man as a big-time brothel-keeper and it was not until we expressed an interest in his finances that the Deuxième Bureau unearthed the parallel dossier which was running with their colleagues of the police department.

The significance of the situation became apparent to us and to our French friends and, in the past few months, a veritable rat-hunt has been operated by the police after the establishments of the Cordon Jaune, with the result that today nothing remains of Le Chiffre's original investment and any routine inquiry would reveal a deficit of around fifty million francs in the trade union funds of which he is the treasurer and paymaster.

It does not seem that the suspicions of Leningrad have been aroused yet but, unfortunately for Le Chiffre, it is possible that at any rate SMERSH is on the scent. Last week a high-grade source of Station P reported that a senior official of this efficient organ of Soviet vengeance had left Warsaw for Strasbourg via the Eastern sector of Berlin. There is no confirmation of this report from the Deuxième Bureau, nor from the authorities in Strasbourg (who are reliable and thorough) and there is also no news from Le Chiffre's headquarters there, which we have well covered by a double agent (in addition to 1860).

If Le Chiffre knew that SMERSH was on his tail or that

they had the smallest suspicion of him, he would have no alternative but to commit suicide or attempt to escape, but his present plans suggest that while he is certainly desperate, he does not yet realize that his life may be at stake. It is these rather spectacular plans of his that have suggested to us a counter-operation which, though risky and unconventional, we submit at the end of this memorandum with confidence.

In brief, Le Chiffre plans, we believe, to follow the example of most other desperate till-robbers and make good the deficit in his accounts by gambling. The 'Bourse' is too slow. So are the various illicit traffics in drugs, or rare medicines, such as aureo- and strepto-mycin and cortisone. No race-tracks could carry the sort of stakes he will have to play and, if he wins, he would more likely be killed than paid off.

In any case, we know that he has withdrawn the final twenty-five million francs from the treasury of his union and that he has taken a small villa in the neighbourhood of Royale-les-Eaux, just north of Dieppe, for a week from a fortnight tomorrow.

Now, it is expected that the Casino at Royale will see the highest gambling in Europe this summer. In an effort to wrest the big money from Deauville and Le Touquet, the Société des Bains de Mers de Royale have leased the baccarat and the two top chemin-de-fer tables to the Mahomet Ali Syndicate, a group of *émigré* Egyptian bankers and business-men with, it is said, a call on certain royal funds, who have for years been trying to cut in on the profits of Zographos and his Greek associates resulting from their monopoly of the highest French baccarat banks.

With the help of discreet publicity, a considerable number of the biggest operators in America and Europe have been encouraged to book at Royale this summer and it seems possible that this old-fashioned watering-place will regain some of its Victorian renown.

Be that as it may, it is here that Le Chiffre will, we are confident, endeavour on or after 15 June to make a profit at baccarat of fifty million francs on a working capital of twenty-five million. (And, incidentally, save his life.)

Proposed Counter-operation

It would be greatly in the interests of this country and of the other nations of the North Atlantic Treaty Organization that this powerful Soviet agent should be ridiculed and destroyed, that his Communist trade union should be bankrupted and brought into disrepute, and that this potential fifth column, with a strength of 50,000, capable in time of war of controlling a wide sector of France's northern frontier, should lose faith and cohesion. All this would result if Le Chiffre could be defeated at the tables. (NB. Assassination is pointless. Leningrad would quickly cover up his defalcations and make him into a martyr.)

We therefore recommend that the finest gambler available to the Service should be given the necessary funds and endeavour to out-gamble this man.

The risks are obvious and the possible loss to the Secret

funds is high, but other operations on which large sums have been hazarded have had fewer chances of success, often for a smaller objective.

If the decision is unfavourable, the only alternative would be to place our information and our recommendations in the hands of the Deuxième Bureau or of our American colleagues of the Central Intelligence Agency in Washington. Both of these organizations would doubtless be delighted to take over the scheme.

Signed: S.

Appendix A.

Name: Le Chiffre.

Aliases: Variations on the words 'cypher' or 'number' in different languages; eg 'Herr Ziffer'.

Origin: Unknown.

First encountered as a displaced person, inmate of Dachau DP camp in the US Zone of Germany, June 1945. Apparently suffering from amnesia and paralysis of vocal cords (? both feigned). Dumbness succumbed to therapy, but subject continued to claim total loss of memory except associations with Alsace-Lorraine and Strasbourg whither he was transferred in September 1945, on Stateless Passport No. 304–596. Adopted the name 'Le Chiffre' ('since I am only a number on a passport'). No Christian names.

Age: About 45.

Description: Height 5 ft 8 ins. Weight 18 stones. Complexion very pale. Clean-shaven. Hair red-brown, 'en brosse'. Eyes very dark brown with whites showing all round iris. Small, rather feminine mouth. False teeth of expensive quality. Ears small, with large lobes, indicating some Jewish blood. Hands small, well-tended, hirsute. Feet small. Racially, subject is probably a mixture of Mediterranean with Prussian or Polish strains. Dresses well and meticulously, generally in dark double-breasted suits. Smokes incessantly Caporals, using a denicotinizing holder. At frequent intervals inhales from benzedrine inhaler. Voice soft and even. Bilingual in French and English. Good German. Traces of Marseilles accent. Smiles infrequently. Does not laugh. *Habits:* Mostly expensive, but discreet. Large sexual appetites. Flagellant. Expert driver of fast cars. Adept with small arms and other forms of personal combat, including knives. Carries three Eversharp razor blades, in hat-band, heel of left shoe and cigarette-case. Knowledge of accountancy and mathematics. Fine gambler. Always accompanied by two armed guards, well-dressed, one French, one German (details available).

Comment: A formidable and dangerous agent of the USSR, controlled by Leningrad Section III through Paris.

Signed: Archivist.

Appendix B.

Subject: SMERSH

Sources: Own archives and scanty material made available by Deuxième Bureau and CIA Washington.

SMERSH is a conjunction of two Russian words:

'Smyert Shpionam', meaning roughly: 'Death to Spies'.

Ranks above MWD (formerly NKVD) and is believed to come under the personal direction of Beria.

Headquarters: Leningrad (sub-station at Moscow).

Its task is the elimination of all forms of treachery and back-sliding with the various branches of the Soviet Secret Service and Secret Police at home and abroad. It is the most powerful and feared organization in the USSR and is popularly believed never to have failed in a mission of vengeance.

It is thought that SMERSH was responsible for the assassination of Trotsky in Mexico (22 August 1940) and may indeed have made its name with this successful murder after attempts by other Russian individuals and organizations had failed.

SMERSH was next heard of when Hitler attacked Russia. It was then rapidly expanded to cope with treachery and double agents during the retreat of the Soviet forces in 1941. At that time it worked as an execution squad for the NKVD and its present selective mission was not so clearly defined.

The organization itself was thoroughly purged after the war and is now believed to consist of only a few hundred operatives of very high quality divided into five sections:

Department I: In charge of counter-intelligence among Soviet organizations at home and abroad.

Department II: Operations, including executions.

Department III: Administration and Finance.

Department IV: Investigations and legal work. Personnel.

Department V: Prosecutions: the section which passes final judgement on all victims.

Only one SMERSH operative has come into our hands since the war: Goytchev, alias Garrad-Jones. He shot Petchora, medical officer at the Yugoslav Embassy, in Hyde Park, 7 August 1948. During interrogation he committed suicide by swallowing a coat-button of compressed potassium cyanide. He revealed nothing beyond his membership of SMERSH, of which he was arrogantly boastful.

We believe that the following British double agents were victims of SMERSH: Donovan, Harthrop-Vane, Elizabeth Dumont, Ventnor, Mace, Savarin. (For details see Morgue: Section Q.)

Conclusion: Every effort should be made to improve our knowledge of this very powerful organization and destroy its operatives.

Head of S (the section of the Secret Service concerned with the Soviet Union) was so keen on his plan for the destruction of Le Chiffre, and it was basically his own plan, that he took the memorandum himself and went up to the top floor of the gloomy building overlooking Regent's Park and through the green baize door and along the corridor to the end room.

He walked belligerently up to M's Chief of Staff, a young sapper who had earned his spurs as one of the secretariat to the Chiefs of Staff committee after having been wounded during a sabotage operation in 1944, and had kept his sense of humour in spite of both experiences.

'Now look here, Bill. I want to sell something to the Chief. Is this a good moment?'

'What do you think, Penny?' The Chief of Staff turned to M's private secretary who shared the room with him.

Miss Moneypenny would have been desirable but for eyes which were cool and direct and quizzical.

'Should be all right. He won a bit of a victory at the FO this morning and he's not got anyone for the next half an hour.' She smiled encouragingly at Head of S whom she liked for himself and for the importance of his section.

'Well, here's the dope, Bill.' He handed over the black folder with the red star which stood for Top Secret. 'And for God's sake look enthusiastic when you give it him. And tell him I'll wait here and read a good code-book while he's considering it. He may want some more details, and anyway I want to see you two don't pester him with anything else until he's finished.'

'All right, sir.' The Chief of Staff pressed a switch and leant towards the intercom on his desk.

'Yes?' asked a quiet, flat voice.

'Head of S has an urgent docket for you, sir.'

There was a pause.

'Bring it in,' said a voice.

The Chief of Staff released the switch and stood up.

'Thanks, Bill. I'll be next door,' said Head of S.

The Chief of Staff crossed his office and went through the double doors leading into M's room. In a moment he came out and over the entrance a small blue light burned the warning that M was not to be disturbed.

Later, a triumphant Head of S said to his Number Two: 'We nearly cooked ourselves with that last paragraph. He said it was subversion and blackmail. He got pretty sharp about it. Anyway, he approves. Says the idea's crazy, but worth trying if the Treasury will play and he thinks they will. He's going to tell them it's a better gamble than the money we're putting into deserting

Russian colonels who turn double after a few months' "asylum" here. And he's longing to get at Le Chiffre, and anyway he's got the right man and wants to try him out on the job.'

'Who is it?' asked Number Two.

'One of the Double Os – I guess 007. He's tough and M thinks there may be trouble with those gunmen of Le Chiffre's. He must be pretty good with the cards or he wouldn't have sat in the Casino in Monte Carlo for two months before the war watching that Roumanian team work their stuff with the invisible ink and the dark glasses. He and the Deuxième bowled them out in the end and 007 turned in a million francs he had won at shemmy. Good money in those days.'

James Bond's interview with M had been short.

'What about it, Bond?' asked M when Bond came back into his room after reading Head of S's memorandum and after gazing for ten minutes out of the waiting-room window at the distant trees in the park.

Bond looked across the desk into the shrewd, clear eyes.

'It's very kind of you, sir, I'd like to do it. But I can't promise to win. The odds at baccarat are the best after *trente-et-quarante* – evens except for the tiny *cagnotte* – but I might get a bad run against me and get cleaned out. Play's going to be pretty high – opening'll go up to half a million, I should think.'

Bond was stopped by the cold eyes. M knew all this

already, knew the odds at baccarat as well as Bond. That was his job – knowing the odds at everything, and knowing men, his own and the opposition's. Bond wished he had kept quiet about his misgivings.

'He can have a bad run too,' said M. 'You'll have plenty of capital. Up to twenty-five million, the same as him. We'll start you on ten and send you another ten when you've had a look round. You can make the extra five yourself.' He smiled. 'Go over a few days before the big game starts and get your hand in. Have a talk to Q about rooms and trains, and any equipment you want. The Paymaster will fix the funds. I'm going to ask the Deuxième to stand by. It's their territory and as it is we shall be lucky if they don't kick up rough. I'll try and persuade them to send Mathis. You seemed to get on well with him in Monte Carlo on that other Casino job. And I'm going to tell Washington because of the NATO angle. CIA have got one or two good men at Fontainebleau with the joint intelligence chaps there. Anything else?'

Bond shook his head. 'I'd certainly like to have Mathis, sir.'

'Well, we'll see. Try and bring it off. We're going to look pretty foolish if you don't. And watch out. This sounds an amusing job, but I don't think it's going to be. Le Chiffre is a good man. Well, best of luck.'

'Thank you, sir,' said Bond and went to the door.

'Just a minute.'

Bond turned.

'I think I'll keep you covered, Bond. Two heads are better than one and you'll need someone to run your communications. I'll think it over. They'll get in touch with you at Royale. You needn't worry. It'll be someone good.'

Bond would have preferred to work alone, but one didn't argue with M. He left the room hoping that the man they sent would be loyal to him and neither stupid, nor, worse still, ambitious.

As two weeks later, James Bond awoke in his room at the Hôtel Splendide, some of this history passed through his mind.

He had arrived at Royale-les-Eaux in time for luncheon two days before. There had been no attempt to contact him and there had been no flicker of curiosity when he had signed the register 'James Bond, Port Maria, Jamaica'.

M had expressed no interest in his cover.

'Once you start to make a set at Le Chiffre at the tables, you'll have had it,' he said. 'But wear a cover that will stick with the general public.'

Bond knew Jamaica well, so he asked to be controlled from there and to pass as a Jamaican plantocrat whose father had made his pile in tobacco and sugar and whose son chose to play it away on the stock markets and in casinos. If inquiries were made, he would quote Charles DaSilva of Chaffery's, Kingston, as his attorney. Charles would make the story stick.

Bond had spent the last two afternoons and most of the nights at the Casino, playing complicated progression systems on the even chances at roulette. He made a high banco at chemin-de-fer whenever he heard one offered. If he lost, he would *suivi* once and not chase it further if he lost the second time.

In this way he had made some three million francs and had given his nerves and card-sense a thorough work-out. He had got the geography of the Casino clear in his mind. Above all, he had been able to observe Le Chiffre at the tables and to note ruefully that he was a faultless and lucky gambler.

Bond liked to make a good breakfast. After a cold shower, he sat at the writing-table in front of the window. He looked out at the beautiful day and consumed half a pint of iced orange juice, three scrambled eggs and bacon and a double portion of coffee without sugar. He lit his first cigarette, a Balkan and Turkish mixture made for him by Morlands of Grosvenor Street, and watched the small waves lick the long seashore and the fishing-fleet from Dieppe string out towards the June heat-haze followed by a paper-chase of herring-gulls.

He was lost in his thoughts when the telephone rang. It was the *concierge* announcing that a Director of Radio Stentor was waiting below with the wireless set he had ordered from Paris.

'Of course,' said Bond. 'Send him up.'

This was the cover fixed by the Deuxième Bureau for their liaison man with Bond. Bond watched the door, hoping that it would be Mathis.

When Mathis came in, a respectable business-man carrying a large square parcel by its leather handle,

Bond smiled broadly and would have greeted him with warmth if Mathis had not frowned and held up his free hand after carefully closing the door.

'I have just arrived from Paris, monsieur, and here is the set you asked to have on approval – five valves, superhet, I think you call it in England, and you should be able to get most of the capitals of Europe from Royale. There are no mountains for forty miles in any direction.'

'It sounds all right,' said Bond, lifting his eyebrows at this mystery-making.

Mathis paid no attention. He placed the set, which he had unwrapped, on the floor beside the unlit panel electric fire below the mantelpiece.

'It is just past eleven,' he said, 'and I see that the Compagnons de la Chanson should now be on the medium wave from Rome. They are touring Europe. Let us see what the reception is like. It should be a fair test.'

He winked. Bond noticed that he had turned the volume on to full and that the red light indicating the long waveband was illuminated, though the set was still silent.

Mathis fiddled at the back of the set. Suddenly an appalling roar of static filled the small room. Mathis gazed at the set for a few seconds with benevolence and then turned it off and his voice was full of dismay.

'My dear monsieur – forgive me please – badly tuned,' and he again bent to the dials. After a few adjustments the close harmony of the French came over the air and Mathis walked up and clapped Bond very hard on the back and wrang his hand until Bond's fingers ached.

Bond smiled back at him. 'Now, what the hell?' he asked.

'My dear friend,' Mathis was delighted, 'you are blown, blown, blown. Up there,' he pointed at the ceiling, 'at this moment, either Monsieur Muntz or his alleged wife, allegedly bedridden with the *grippe*, is deafened, absolutely deafened, and I hope in agony.' He grinned with pleasure at Bond's frown of disbelief.

Mathis sat down on the bed and ripped open a packet of Caporal with his thumbnail. Bond waited.

Mathis was satisfied with the sensation his words had caused. He became serious.

'How it has happened I don't know. They must have been on to you for several days before you arrived. The opposition is here in real strength. Above you is the Muntz family. He is German. She is from somewhere in Central Europe, perhaps a Czech. This is an old-fashioned hotel. There are disused chimneys behind these electric fires. Just here,' he pointed a few inches above the panel fire, 'is suspended a very powerful radio pick-up. The wires run up the chimney to behind the Muntzes' electric fire where there is an amplifier. In their room is a wire-recorder and a pair of earphones on which the Muntzes listen in turn. That is why

Madame Muntz has the *grippe* and takes all her meals in bed and why Monsieur Muntz has to be constantly at her side instead of enjoying the sunshine and the gambling of this delightful resort.

'Some of this we knew because in France we are very clever. The rest we confirmed by unscrewing your electric fire a few hours before you got here.'

Suspiciously Bond walked over and examined the screws which secured the panel to the wall. Their grooves showed minute scratches.

'Now it is time for a little more play-acting,' said Mathis. He walked over to the radio, which was still transmitting close harmony to its audience of three, and switched it off.

'Are you satisfied, monsieur?' he asked. 'You notice how clearly they came over. Are they not a wonderful team?' He made a winding motion with his right hand and raised his eyebrows.

'They are so good,' said Bond, 'that I would like to hear the rest of the programme.' He grinned at the thought of the angry glances which the Muntzes must be exchanging overhead. 'The machine itself seems splendid. Just what I was looking for to take back to Jamaica.'

Mathis made a sarcastic grimace and switched back to the Rome programme.

'You and your Jamaica,' he said, and sat down again on the bed.

Bond frowned at him. 'Well, it's no good crying over

spilt milk,' he said. 'We didn't expect the cover to stick for long, but it's worrying that they bowled it out so soon.' He searched his mind in vain for a clue. Could the Russians have broken one of our ciphers? If so, he might just as well pack up and go home. He and his job would have been stripped naked.

Mathis seemed to read his mind. 'It can't have been a cipher,' he said. 'Anyway, we told London at once and they will have changed them. A pretty flap we caused, I can tell you.' He smiled with the satisfaction of a friendly rival. 'And now to business, before our good "Compagnons" run out of breath.

'First of all,' and he inhaled a thick lungful of Caporal, 'you will be pleased with your Number Two. She is very beautiful' – Bond frowned – 'very beautiful indeed.' Satisfied with Bond's reaction, Mathis continued: 'She has black hair, blue eyes, and splendid . . . er . . . protuberances. Back and front,' he added. 'And she is a wireless expert which, though sexually less interesting, makes her a perfect employee of Radio Stentor and assistant to myself in my capacity as wireless salesman for this rich summer season down here.' He grinned. 'We are both staying in the hotel and my assistant will thus be on hand in case your new radio breaks down. All new machines, even French ones, are apt to have teething troubles in the first day or two. And occasionally at night,' he added with an exaggerated wink.

Bond was not amused. 'What the hell do they want

to send me a woman for?' he said bitterly. 'Do they think this is a bloody picnic?'

Mathis interrupted. 'Calm yourself, my dear James. She is as serious as you could wish and as cold as an icicle. She speaks French like a native and knows her job backwards. Her cover's perfect and I have arranged for her to team up with you quite smoothly. What is more natural than that you should pick up a pretty girl here? As a Jamaican millionaire,' he coughed respectfully, 'what with your hot blood and all, you would look naked without one.'

Bond grunted dubiously.

'Any other surprises?' he asked suspiciously.

'Nothing very much,' answered Mathis. 'Le Chiffre is installed in his villa. It's about ten miles down the coast road. He has his two guards with him. They look pretty capable fellows. One of them has been seen visiting a little "pension" in the town where three mysterious and rather subhuman characters checked in two days ago. They may be part of the team. Their papers are in order – stateless Czechs apparently – but one of our men says the language they talk in their room is Bulgarian. We don't see many of those around. They're mostly used against the Turks and the Yugoslavs. They're stupid, but obedient. The Russians use them for simple killings or as fall-guys for more complicated ones.'

'Thanks very much. Which is mine to be?' asked Bond. 'Anything else?'

'No. Come to the bar of the Hermitage before lunch. I'll fix the introduction. Ask her to dinner this evening. Then it will be natural for her to come into the Casino with you. I'll be there too, but in the background. I've got one or two good chaps and we'll keep an eye on you. Oh, and there's an American called Leiter here, staying in the hotel. Felix Leiter. He's the CIA chap from Fontainebleau. London told me to tell you. He looks okay. May come in useful.'

A torrent of Italian burst from the wireless set on the floor. Mathis switched it off and they exchanged some phrases about the set and about how Bond should pay for it. Then with effusive farewells and a final wink Mathis bowed himself out.

Bond sat at the window and gathered his thoughts. Nothing that Mathis had told him was reassuring. He was completely blown and under really professional surveillance. An attempt might be made to put him away before he had a chance to pit himself against Le Chiffre at the tables. The Russians had no stupid prejudices about murder. And then there was this pest of a girl. He sighed. Women were for recreation. On a job, they got in the way and fogged things up with sex and hurt feelings and all the emotional baggage they carried around. One had to look out for them and take care of them.

'Bitch,' said Bond, and then remembering the Muntzes, he said 'bitch' again more loudly and walked out of the room.

It was twelve o'clock when Bond left the Splendide and the clock on the *mairie* was stumbling through its midday carillon. There was a strong scent of pine and mimosa in the air and the freshly watered gardens of the Casino opposite, interspersed with neat gravel parterres and paths, lent the scene a pretty formalism more appropriate to ballet than to melodrama.

The sun shone and there was a gaiety and sparkle in the air which seemed to promise well for the new era of fashion and prosperity for which the little seaside town, after many vicissitudes, was making its gallant bid.

Royale-les-Eaux, which lies near the mouth of the Somme before the flat coast-line soars up from the beaches of southern Picardy to the Brittany cliffs which run on to Le Havre, had experienced much the same fortunes as Trouville.

Royale (without the 'Eaux') also started as a small fishing village and its rise to fame as a fashionable watering-place during the Second Empire was as meteoric as that of Trouville. But as Deauville killed Trouville, so, after a long period of decline, did Le Touquet kill Royale.

At the turn of the century, when things were going badly for the little seaside town and when the fashion was to combine pleasure with a 'cure', a natural spring in the hills behind Royale was discovered to contain enough diluted sulphur to have a beneficent effect on the liver. Since all French people suffer from liver complaints, Royale quickly became 'Royale-les-Eaux', and 'Eau Royale', in a torpedo-shaped bottle, grafted itself demurely on to the tail of the mineral-water lists in hotels and restaurant cars.

It did not long withstand the powerful combines of Vichy and Perrier and Vittel. There came a series of lawsuits, a number of people lost a lot of money and very soon its sale was again entirely local. Royale fell back on the takings from the French and English families during the summer, on its fishing-fleet in winter and on the crumbs which fell to its elegantly dilapidated Casino from the table at Le Touquet.

But there was something splendid about the Negresco baroque of the Casino Royale, a strong whiff of Victorian elegance and luxury, and in 1950 Royale caught the fancy of a syndicate in Paris which disposed of large funds belonging to a group of expatriate Vichyites.

Brighton had been revived since the war, and Nice. Nostalgia for more spacious, golden times might be a source of revenue.

The Casino was repainted in its original white and gilt and the rooms decorated in the palest grey with wine-red carpets and curtains. Vast chandeliers were suspended from the ceilings. The gardens were spruced and the fountains played again and the two main hotels, the Splendide and the Hermitage, were prinked and furbished and restaffed.

Even the small town and the *vieux-port* managed to fix welcoming smiles across their ravaged faces, and the main street became gay with the *vitrines* of great Paris jewellers and couturiers, tempted down for a butterfly season by rent-free sites and lavish promises.

Then the Mahomet Ali Syndicate was cajoled into starting a high game in the Casino and the Société des Bains de Mer de Royale felt that now at last Le Touquet would have to yield up some of the treasure stolen over the years from its parent *plage*.

Against the background of this luminous and sparkling stage Bond stood in the sunshine and felt his mission to be incongruous and remote and his dark profession an affront to his fellow actors.

He shrugged away the momentary feeling of unease and walked round the back of his hotel and down the ramp to the garage. Before his rendezvous at the Hermitage he decided to take his car down the coast road and have a quick look at Le Chiffre's villa and then drive back by the inland road until it crossed the *route nationale* to Paris.

Bond's car was his only personal hobby. One of the last of the $4\frac{1}{2}$-litre Bentleys with the supercharger by Amherst Villiers, he had bought it almost new in 1933 and had kept it in careful storage through the war. It was still serviced every year and, in London, a former Bentley mechanic, who worked in a garage near Bond's Chelsea flat, tended it with jealous care. Bond drove it hard and well and with an almost sensual pleasure. It was a battleship-grey convertible coupé, which really did convert, and it was capable of touring at ninety with thirty miles an hour in reserve.

Bond eased the car out of the garage and up the ramp and soon the loitering drum-beat of the two-inch exhaust was echoing down the tree-lined boulevard, through the crowded main street of the little town, and off through the sand dunes to the south.

An hour later, Bond walked into the Hermitage bar and chose a table near one of the broad windows.

The room was sumptuous with those over-masculine trappings which, together with briar pipes and wire-haired terriers, spell luxury in France. Everything was brass-studded leather and polished mahogany. The curtains and carpets were in royal blue. The waiters wore striped waistcoats and green baize aprons. Bond ordered an Americano and examined the sprinkling of over-dressed customers, mostly from Paris he guessed, who sat talking with focus and vivacity, creating that theatrically clubbable atmosphere of *l'heure de l'apéritif.*

The men were drinking inexhaustible quarter-bottles of champagne, the women dry martinis.

'*Moi, j'adore le "Dry"*,' a bright-faced girl at the next

table said to her companion, too neat in his unseason-able tweeds, who gazed at her with moist brown eyes over the top of an expensive shooting-stick from Hermes, '*fait avec du Gordon's, bien entendu.*'

'*D'accord, Daisy. Mais tu sais, un zeste de citron . . .*'

Bond's eye was caught by the tall figure of Mathis on the pavement outside, his face turned in animation to a dark-haired girl in grey. His arm was linked in hers, high up above the elbow, and yet there was a lack of intimacy in their appearance, an ironical chill in the girl's profile, which made them seem two separate people rather than a couple. Bond waited for them to come through the street door into the bar, but for appearances' sake continued to stare out of the window at the passers-by.

'But surely it is Monsieur Bond?' Mathis's voice behind him was full of surprised delight. Bond, appro-priately flustered, rose to his feet. 'Can it be that you are alone? Are you awaiting someone? May I present my colleague, Mademoiselle Lynd? My dear, this is the gentleman from Jamaica with whom I had the pleasure of doing business this morning.'

Bond inclined himself with a reserved friendliness. 'It would be a great pleasure,' he addressed himself to the girl. 'I am alone. Would you both care to join me?' He pulled out a chair and while they sat down he beckoned to a waiter and despite Mathis's expostula-tions insisted on ordering the drinks – a *fine à l'eau* for Mathis and a Bacardi for the girl.

Mathis and Bond exchanged cheerful talk about the fine weather and the prospects of a revival in the fortunes of Royale-les-Eaux. The girl sat silent. She accepted one of Bond's cigarettes, examined it and then smoked it appreciatively and without affectation, drawing the smoke deeply into her lungs with a little sigh and then exhaling it casually through her lips and nostrils. Her movements were economical and precise with no trace of self-consciousness.

Bond felt her presence strongly. While he and Mathis talked, he turned from time to time towards her, politely including her in the conversation, but adding up the impressions recorded by each glance.

Her hair was very black and she wore it cut square and low on the nape of the neck, framing her face to below the clear and beautiful line of her jaw. Although it was heavy and moved with the movements of her head, she did not constantly pat it back into place, but let it alone. Her eyes were wide apart and deep blue and they gazed candidly back at Bond with a touch of ironical disinterest which, to his annoyance, he found he would like to shatter, roughly. Her skin was lightly sun-tanned and bore no trace of make-up except on her mouth which was wide and sensual. Her bare arms and hands had a quality of repose and the general impression of restraint in her appearance and movements was carried even to her fingernails which were unpainted and cut short. Round her neck she wore a plain gold chain of wide flat links and on the fourth finger of the right hand a broad topaz ring. Her medium-length dress was of grey *soie sauvage* with a square-cut bodice, lasciviously tight across her fine breasts. The skirt was closely pleated and flowered down from a narrow, but not a thin, waist. She wore a three-inch, handstitched black belt. A handstitched black *sabretache* rested on the chair beside her, together with a wide cart-wheel hat of gold straw, its crown encircled by a thin black velvet ribbon which tied at the back in a short bow. Her shoes were square-toed of plain black leather.

Bond was excited by her beauty and intrigued by her composure. The prospect of working with her stimulated him. At the same time he felt a vague disquiet. On an impulse he touched wood.

Mathis had noticed Bond's preoccupation. After a time he rose.

'Forgive me,' he said to the girl, 'while I telephone to the Dubernes. I must arrange my rendezvous for dinner tonight. Are you sure you won't mind being left to your own devices this evening?'

She shook her head.

Bond took the cue and, as Mathis crossed the room to the telephone booth beside the bar, he said: 'If you are going to be alone tonight, would you care to have dinner with me?'

She smiled with the first hint of conspiracy she had shown. 'I would like to very much,' she said, 'and then perhaps you would chaperon me to the Casino where

Monsieur Mathis tells me you are very much at home. Perhaps I will bring you luck.'

With Mathis gone, her attitude towards him showed a sudden warmth. She seemed to acknowledge that they were a team and, as they discussed the time and place of their meeting, Bond realized that it would be quite easy after all to plan the details of his project with her. He felt that after all she was interested and excited by her role and that she would work willingly with him. He had imagined many hurdles before establishing a rapport, but now he felt he could get straight down to professional details. He was quite honest to himself about the hypocrisy of his attitude towards her. As a woman, he wanted to sleep with her but only when the job had been done.

When Mathis came back to the table Bond called for his bill. He explained that he was expected back at his hotel to have lunch with friends. When for a moment he held her hand in his he felt a warmth of affection and understanding pass between them that would have seemed impossible half an hour earlier.

The girl's eyes followed him out on to the boulevard.

Mathis moved his chair close to hers and said softly: 'That is a very good friend of mine. I am glad you have met each other. I can already feel the ice-floes on the two rivers breaking up.' He smiled, 'I don't think Bond has ever been melted. It will be a new experience for him. And for you.'

She did not answer him directly.

'He is very good-looking. He reminds me rather of Hoagy Carmichael, but there is something cold and ruthless in his . . .'

The sentence was never finished. Suddenly a few feet away the entire plate-glass window shivered into confetti. The blast of a terrific explosion, very near, hit them so that they were rocked back in their chairs. There was an instant of silence. Some objects pattered down on to the pavement outside. Bottles slowly toppled off the shelves behind the bar. Then there were screams and a stampede for the door.

'Stay there,' said Mathis.

He kicked back his chair and hurtled through the empty window-frame on to the pavement.

When Bond left the bar he walked purposefully along the pavement flanking the tree-lined boulevard towards his hotel a few hundred yards away. He was hungry.

The day was still beautiful, but by now the sun was very hot and the plane-trees, spaced about twenty feet apart on the grass verge between the pavement and the broad tarmac, gave a cool shade.

There were few people abroad and the two men standing quietly under a tree on the opposite side of the boulevard looked out of place.

Bond noticed them when he was still a hundred yards away and when the same distance separated them from the ornamental *porte cochère* of the Splendide.

There was something rather disquieting about their appearance. They were both small and they were dressed alike in dark and, Bond reflected, rather hot-looking suits. They had the appearance of a variety turn waiting for a bus on the way to the theatre. Each wore a straw hat with a thick black ribbon as a concession, perhaps, to the holiday atmosphere of the resort, and the brims of these and the shadow from the tree

under which they stood obscured their faces. Incongru-
ously, each dark, squat little figure was illuminated by
a touch of bright colour. They were both carrying square
camera-cases slung from the shoulder.

And one case was bright red and the other case bright
blue.

By the time Bond had taken in these details, he had
come to within fifty yards of the two men. He was
reflecting on the ranges of various types of weapon and
the possibilities of cover when an extraordinary and
terrible scene was enacted.

Red-man seemed to give a short nod to Blue-man.
With a quick movement Blue-man unslung his blue
camera-case. Blue-man, and Bond could not see exactly
as the trunk of a plane-tree beside him just then inter-
vened to obscure his vision, bent forward and seemed
to fiddle with the case. Then with a blinding flash
of white light there was the ear-splitting crack of a
monstrous explosion and Bond, despite the protection
of the tree-trunk, was slammed down to the pavement
by a bolt of hot air which dented his cheeks and
stomach as if they had been made of paper. He lay,
gazing up at the sun, while the air (or so it seemed to
him) went on twanging with the explosion as if
someone had hit the bass register of a piano with a
sledgehammer.

When, dazed and half-conscious, he raised himself
on one knee, a ghastly rain of pieces of flesh and shreds
of blood-soaked clothing fell on him and around him,

mingled with branches and gravel. Then a shower of small twigs and leaves. From all sides came the sharp tinkle of falling glass. Above in the sky hung a mushroom of black smoke which rose and dissolved as he drunkenly watched it. There was an obscene smell of high explosive, of burning wood, and of, yes, that was it – roast mutton. For fifty yards down the boulevard the trees were leafless and charred. Opposite, two of them had snapped off near the base and lay drunkenly across the road. Between them there was a still smoking crater. Of the two men in straw hats, there remained absolutely nothing. But there were red traces on the road, and on the pavements and against the trunks of the trees, and there were glittering shreds high up in the branches.

Bond felt himself starting to vomit.

It was Mathis who got to him first, and by that time Bond was standing with his arm round the tree which had saved his life.

Stupefied, but unharmed, he allowed Mathis to lead him off towards the Splendide from which guests and servants were pouring in chattering fright. As the distant clang of bells heralded the arrival of ambulances and fire-engines, they managed to push through the throng and up the short stairs and along the corridor to Bond's room.

Mathis paused only to turn on the radio in front of the fireplace, then, while Bond stripped off his blood-flecked clothes, Mathis sprayed him with questions.

When it came to the description of the two men, Mathis tore the telephone off its hook beside Bond's bed.

' . . . and tell the police,' he concluded, 'tell them that the Englishman from Jamaica who was knocked over by the blast is my affair. He is unhurt and they are not to worry him. I will explain to them in half an hour. They should tell the Press that it was apparently a vendetta between two Bulgarian Communists and that one killed the other with a bomb. They need say nothing of the third Bulgar who must have been hanging about somewhere, but they must get him at all costs. He will certainly head for Paris. Road-blocks everywhere. Understand? *Alors, bonne chance.*'

Mathis turned back to Bond and heard him to the end.

'*Merde*, but you were lucky,' he said when Bond had finished. 'Clearly the bomb was intended for you. It must have been faulty. They intended to throw it and then dodge behind their tree. But it all came out the other way round. Never mind. We will discover the facts.' He paused. 'But certainly it is a curious affair. And these people appear to be taking you seriously.' Mathis looked affronted. 'But how did these *sacré* Bulgars intend to escape capture? And what was the significance of the red and the blue cases? We must try and find some fragments of the red one.'

Mathis bit his nails. He was excited and his eyes

glittered. This was becoming a formidable and dramatic affair, in many aspects of which he was now involved personally. Certainly it was no longer just a case of holding Bond's coat while he had his private battle with Le Chiffre in the Casino. Mathis jumped up.

'Now get a drink and some lunch and a rest,' he ordered Bond. 'For me, I must get my nose quickly into this affair before the police have muddied the trail with their big black boots.'

Mathis turned off the radio and waved an affectionate farewell. The door slammed and silence settled on the room. Bond sat for a while by the window and enjoyed being alive.

Later, as Bond was finishing his first straight whisky 'on the rocks' and was contemplating the *paté de foie gras* and cold *langouste* which the waiter had just laid out for him, the telephone rang.

'This is Mademoiselle Lynd.'

The voice was low and anxious.

'Are you all right?'

'Yes, quite.'

'I'm glad. Please take care of yourself.'

She rang off.

Bond shook himself, then he picked up his knife and selected the thickest of the pieces of hot toast.

He suddenly thought: two of them are dead, and I have got one more on my side. It's a start.

He dipped the knife into the glass of very hot water

which stood beside the pot of Strasbourg porcelain and reminded himself to tip the waiter doubly for this particular meal.

Bond was determined to be completely fit and relaxed for a gambling session which might last most of the night. He ordered a masseur for three o'clock. After the remains of his luncheon had been removed, he sat at his window gazing out to sea until there came a knock on the door as the masseur, a Swede, presented himself.

Silently he got to work on Bond from his feet to his neck, melting the tensions in his body and calming his still twanging nerves. Even the long purpling bruises down Bond's left shoulder and side ceased to throb, and when the Swede had gone Bond fell into a dreamless sleep.

He awoke in the evening completely refreshed.

After a cold shower, Bond walked over to the Casino. Since the night before he had lost the mood of the tables. He needed to re-establish that focus which is half mathematical and half intuitive and which, with a slow pulse and a sanguine temperament, Bond knew to be the essential equipment of any gambler who was set on winning.

Bond had always been a gambler. He loved the dry riffle of the cards and the constant unemphatic drama of the quiet figures round the green tables. He liked the solid, studied comfort of card-rooms and casinos, the well-padded arms of the chairs, the glass of champagne or whisky at the elbow, the quiet unhurried attention of good servants. He was amused by the impartiality of the roulette ball and of the playing-cards – and their eternal bias. He liked being an actor and a spectator and from his chair to take part in other men's dramas and decisions, until it came to his own turn to say that vital 'yes' or 'no', generally on a fifty-fifty chance.

Above all, he liked it that everything was one's own fault. There was only oneself to praise or blame. Luck was a servant and not a master. Luck had to be accepted with a shrug or taken advantage of up to the hilt. But it had to be understood and recognized for what it was and not confused with a faulty appreciation of the odds, for, at gambling, the deadly sin is to mistake bad play for bad luck. And luck in all its moods had to be loved and not feared. Bond saw luck as a woman, to be softly wooed or brutally ravaged, never pandered to or pursued. But he was honest enough to admit that he had never yet been made to suffer by cards or by women. One day, and he accepted the fact, he would be brought to his knees by love or by luck. When that happened he knew that he too would be branded with the deadly question-mark he recognized so often in others, the promise to pay before you have lost: the acceptance of fallibility.

But on this June evening when Bond walked through the 'kitchen' into the *salle privée*, it was with a sensation of confidence and cheerful anticipation that he changed a million francs into plaques of fifty mille and took a seat next to the *chef de partie* at Roulette Table Number 1.

Bond borrowed the *chef*'s card and studied the run of the ball since the session had started at three o'clock that afternoon. He always did this although he knew that each turn of the wheel, each fall of the ball into a numbered slot, has absolutely no connexion with its predecessor. He accepted that the game begins afresh each time the croupier picks up the ivory ball with his right hand, gives one of the four spokes of the wheel a controlled twist clockwise with the same hand, and with a third motion, also with the right hand, flicks the ball round the outer rim of the wheel anticlockwise, against the spin.

It was obvious that all this ritual and all the mechanical minutiae of the wheel, of the numbered slots and the cylinder, had been devised and perfected over the years so that neither the skill of the croupier nor any bias in the wheel could affect the fall of the ball. And yet it is a convention among roulette players, and Bond rigidly adhered to it, to take careful note of the past history of each session and to be guided by any peculiarities in the run of the wheel. To note, for instance, and consider significant, sequences of more than two on a single number or of more than four at the other chances down to evens.

Bond didn't defend the practice. He simply maintained that the more effort and ingenuity you put into gambling, the more you took out.

On the record of that particular table, after about three hours' play, Bond could see little of interest except that the last dozen had been out of favour. It was his practice to play always with the wheel, and only to turn against its previous pattern and start on a new tack after a zero had turned up. So he decided to play one of his favourite gambits and back two – in this case the first two – dozens, each with the maximum – one hundred thousand francs. He thus had two-thirds of the board covered (less the zero) and, since the dozens pay odds of two to one, he stood to win a hundred thousand francs every time any number lower than twenty-five turned up.

After seven coups he had won six times. He lost on the seventh when thirty came up. His net profit was four hundred thousand francs. He kept off the table for the eighth throw. Zero turned up. This piece of luck cheered him further and, accepting the thirty as a fingerpost to the last dozen, he decided to back the first and last dozens until he had lost twice. Ten throws later the middle dozen came up twice, costing him four hundred thousand francs, but he rose from the table one million francs to the good.

Directly Bond had started playing in maximums, his game had become the centre of interest at the table. As he seemed to be in luck, one or two pilot fish started to swim with the shark. Sitting directly opposite, one of these, whom Bond took to be an American, had shown more than the usual friendliness and pleasure at his share of the winning streak. He had smiled once or twice across the table, and there was something pointed in the way he duplicated Bond's movements, placing his two modest plaques of ten mille exactly opposite Bond's larger ones. When Bond rose, he too pushed back his chair and called cheerfully across the table:

'Thanks for the ride. Guess I owe you a drink. Will you join me?'

Bond had a feeling that this might be the CIA man. He knew he was right as they strolled off together towards the bar, after Bond had thrown a plaque of ten mille to the croupier and had given a mille to the *huissier* who drew back his chair.

'My name's Felix Leiter,' said the American. 'Glad to meet you.'

'Mine's Bond – James Bond.'

'Oh yes,' said his companion, 'and now let's see. What shall we have to celebrate?'

Bond insisted on ordering Leiter's Haig-and-Haig 'on the rocks' and then he looked carefully at the barman.

'A dry martini,' he said. 'One. In a deep champagne goblet.'

'*Oui, monsieur.*'

'Just a moment. Three measures of Gordon's, one of vodka, half a measure of Kina Lillet. Shake it very well until it's ice-cold, then add a large thin slice of lemon-peel. Got it?'

'Certainly, monsieur.' The barman seemed pleased with the idea.

'Gosh, that's certainly a drink,' said Leiter.

Bond laughed. 'When I'm . . . er . . . concentrating,' he explained, 'I never have more than one drink before dinner. But I do like that one to be large and very strong and very cold and very well-made. I hate small portions of anything, particularly when they taste bad. This drink's my own invention. I'm going to patent it when I can think of a good name.'

He watched carefully as the deep glass became frosted with the pale golden drink, slightly aerated by the bruising of the shaker. He reached for it and took a long sip.

'Excellent,' he said to the barman, 'but if you can get a vodka made with grain instead of potatoes, you will find it still better.'

'*Mais n'enculons pas des mouches*,' he added in an aside to the barman. The barman grinned.

'That's a vulgar way of saying "we won't split hairs",' explained Bond.

But Leiter was still interested in Bond's drink. 'You certainly think things out,' he said with amusement as they carried their glasses to a corner of the room. He lowered his voice.

'You'd better call it the "Molotov Cocktail" after the one you tasted this afternoon.'

They sat down. Bond laughed.

'I see that the spot marked "X" has been roped off and they're making cars take a detour over the pavement. I hope it hasn't frightened away any of the big money.'

'People are accepting the Communist story or else they think it was a burst gas-main. All the burnt trees are coming down tonight and if they work things here like they do at Monte Carlo, there won't be a trace of the mess left in the morning.'

Leiter shook a Chesterfield out of his pack. 'I'm glad to be working with you on this job,' he said, looking into his drink, 'so I'm particularly glad you didn't get blown to glory. Our people are definitely interested. They think it's just as important as your friends do and they don't think there's anything crazy about it at all. In fact, Washington's pretty sick we're not running the show, but you know what the big brass is like. I expect your fellows are much the same in London.'

Bond nodded. 'Apt to be a bit jealous of their scoops,' he admitted.

'Anyway, I'm under your orders and I'm to give you any help you ask for. With Mathis and his boys here, there may not be much that isn't taken care of already. But, anyway, here I am.'

'I'm delighted you are,' said Bond. 'The opposition has got me, and probably you and Mathis too, all weighed up and it seems no holds are going to be barred. I'm glad Le Chiffre seems as desperate as we thought he was. I'm afraid I haven't got anything very specific for you to do, but I'd be grateful if you'd stick around the Casino this evening. I've got an assistant, a Miss Lynd, and I'd like to hand her over to you when I start playing. You won't be ashamed of her. She's a good-looking girl.' He smiled at Leiter. 'And you might mark his two gunmen. I can't imagine he'll try a rough house, but you never know.'

'I may be able to help,' said Leiter. 'I was a regular in our Marine Corps before I joined this racket, if that means anything to you.' He looked at Bond with a hint of self-deprecation.

'It does,' said Bond.

It turned out that Leiter was from Texas. While he talked on about his job with the Joint Intelligence Staff of NATO and the difficulty of maintaining security in an organization where so many nationalities were represented, Bond reflected that good Americans were fine people and that most of them seemed to come from Texas.

Felix Leiter was about thirty-five. He was tall with a thin bony frame and his lightweight, tan-coloured suit hung loosely from his shoulders like the clothes of Frank Sinatra. His movements and speech were slow, but one had the feeling that there was plenty of speed and strength in him and that he would be a tough and cruel fighter. As he sat hunched over the table, he seemed to have some of the jack-knife quality of a falcon. There was this impression also in his face, in the sharpness of his chin and cheekbones and the wide wry mouth. His grey eyes had a feline slant which was increased by his habit of screwing them up against the smoke of the Chesterfields which he tapped out of the pack in a chain. The permanent wrinkles which this habit had etched at the corners gave the impression that he smiled more with his eyes than with his mouth. A mop of straw-coloured hair lent his face a boyish look which closer examination contradicted. Although he seemed to talk quite openly about his duties in Paris, Bond soon noticed that he never spoke of his American colleagues in Europe or in Washington and he guessed that Leiter held the interests of his own organization far above the mutual concerns of the North Atlantic Allies. Bond sympathized with him.

By the time Leiter had swallowed another whisky and Bond had told him about the Muntzes and his short reconnaissance trip down the coast that morning, it was seven-thirty, and they decided to stroll over to their hotel together. Before leaving the Casino, Bond deposited his total capital of twenty-four million at the *caisse*, keeping only a few notes of ten mille as pocket money.

As they walked across to the Splendide, they saw that a team of workmen was already busy at the scene of the explosion. Several trees were uprooted and hoses from three municipal tank cars were washing down the boulevard and pavements. The bomb-crater had disappeared and only a few passers-by had paused to gape. Bond assumed that similar face-lifting had already been carried out at the Hermitage and to the shops and frontages which had lost their windows.

In the warm blue dusk Royale-les-Eaux was once again orderly and peaceful.

'Who's the *concierge* working for?' asked Leiter as they approached the hotel. Bond was not sure, and said so.

Mathis had been unable to enlighten him. 'Unless you have bought him yourself,' he had said, 'you must assume that he has been bought by the other side. All *concierges* are venal. It is not their fault. They are trained to regard all hotel guests except maharajahs as potential cheats and thieves. They have as much concern for your comfort or well-being as crocodiles.'

Bond remembered Mathis's pronouncement when the *concierge* hurried up to inquire whether he had recovered from his most unfortunate experience of the afternoon. Bond thought it well to say that he still felt a little shaky. He hoped that if the intelligence were relayed, Le Chiffre would at any rate start playing that evening with a basic misinterpretation of his adversary's strength. The *concierge* proffered glycerine hopes for Bond's recovery.

Leiter's room was on one of the upper floors and they parted company at the lift after arranging to see each other at the Casino at around half past ten or eleven, the usual hour for the high tables to begin play.

Bond walked up to his room, which again showed no sign of trespass, threw off his clothes, took a long hot bath followed by an ice-cold shower and lay down on his bed. There remained an hour in which to rest and compose his thoughts before he met the girl in the Splendide bar, an hour to examine minutely the details of his plans for the game, and for after the game, in all the various circumstances of victory or defeat. He had to plan the attendant roles of Mathis, Leiter, and the girl and visualize the reactions of the enemy in various contingencies. He closed his eyes and his thoughts pursued his imagination through a series of carefully constructed scenes as if he was watching the tumbling chips of coloured glass in a kaleidoscope.

At twenty minutes to nine he had exhausted all the permutations which might result from his duel with Le Chiffre. He rose and dressed, dismissing the future completely from his mind.

As he tied his thin, double-ended, black satin tie, he paused for a moment and examined himself levelly in the mirror. His grey-blue eyes looked calmly back with a hint of ironical inquiry and the short lock of black hair which would never stay in place slowly subsided to form a thick comma above his right eyebrow. With the thin vertical scar down his right cheek the general effect was faintly piratical. Not much of Hoagy Carmichael there, thought Bond, as he filled a flat, light gunmetal box with fifty of the Morland cigarettes with the triple gold band. Mathis had told him of the girl's comment.

He slipped the case into his hip pocket and snapped his oxidized Ronson to see if it needed fuel. After pocketing the thin sheaf of ten-mille notes, he opened a drawer and took out a light chamois leather holster and slipped it over his left shoulder so that it hung about three inches below his arm-pit. He then took from under his shirts in another drawer a very flat .25 Beretta automatic with a skeleton grip, extracted the clip and the single round in the barrel and whipped the action to and fro several times, finally pulling the trigger on the empty chamber. He charged the weapon again, loaded it, put up the safety catch and dropped it into the shallow pouch of the shoulder-holster. He looked carefully round the room to see if anything had been forgotten and slipped his single-breasted dinner-jacket coat over his heavy silk evening shirt. He felt cool and comfortable. He verified in the mirror that there was absolutely no sign of the flat gun under his left arm, gave a final pull at his narrow tie and walked out of the door and locked it.

When he turned at the foot of the short stairs towards

the bar he heard the lift-door open behind him and a cool voice call 'Good evening'.

It was the girl. She stood and waited for him to come up to her.

He had remembered her beauty exactly. He was not surprised to be thrilled by it again.

Her dress was of black velvet, simple and yet with the touch of splendour that only half a dozen *couturiers* in the world can achieve. There was a thin necklace of diamonds at her throat and a diamond clip in the low vee which just exposed the jutting swell of her breasts. She carried a plain black evening bag, a flat object which she now held, her arm akimbo, at her waist. Her jet black hair hung straight and simple to the final inward curl below the chin.

She looked quite superb and Bond's heart lifted.

'You look absolutely lovely. Business must be good in the radio world!'

She put her arm through his. 'Do you mind if we go straight into dinner?' she asked. 'I want to make a grand entrance and the truth is there's a horrible secret about black velvet. It marks when you sit down. And, by the way, if you hear me scream tonight, I shall have sat on a cane chair.'

Bond laughed. 'Of course, let's go straight in. We'll have a glass of vodka while we order our dinner.'

She gave him an amused glance and he corrected himself: 'Or a cocktail, of course, if you prefer it. The food here's the best in Royale.'

For an instant he felt nettled at the irony, the light shadow of a snub, with which she had met his decisiveness, and at the way he had risen to her quick glance.

But it was only an infinitesimal clink of foils and as the bowing *maître d'hôtel* led them through the crowded room, it was forgotten as Bond in her wake watched the heads of the diners turn to look at her.

The fashionable part of the restaurant was beside the wide crescent of window built out like the broad stern of a ship over the hotel gardens, but Bond had chosen a table in one of the mirrored alcoves at the back of the great room. These had survived from the Edwardian days and they were secluded and gay in white and gilt, with the red silk-shaded table and wall lights of the late Empire.

As they deciphered the maze of purple ink which covered the double folio menu, Bond beckoned to the *sommelier*. He turned to his companion.

'Have you decided?'

'I would love a glass of vodka,' she said simply, and went back to her study of the menu.

'A small carafe of vodka, very cold,' ordered Bond. He said to her abruptly: 'I can't drink the health of your new frock without knowing your Christian name.'

'Vesper,' she said. 'Vesper Lynd.'

Bond gave her a look of inquiry.

'It's rather a bore always having to explain, but I was born in the evening, on a very stormy evening according to my parents. Apparently they wanted to remember it.' She smiled. 'Some people like it, others don't. I'm just used to it.'

'I think it's a fine name,' said Bond. An idea struck him. 'Can I borrow it?' He explained about the special martini he had invented and his search for a name for it. 'The Vesper,' he said. 'It sounds perfect and it's very appropriate to the violet hour when my cocktail will now be drunk all over the world. Can I have it?'

'So long as I can try one first,' she promised. 'It sounds a drink to be proud of.'

'We'll have one together when all this is finished,' said Bond. 'Win or lose. And now have you decided what you would like to have for dinner? Please be expensive,' he added as he sensed her hesitation, 'or you'll let down that beautiful frock.'

'I'd made two choices,' she laughed, 'and either would have been delicious, but behaving like a millionaire occasionally is a wonderful treat and if you're sure ... well, I'd like to start with caviar and then have a plain grilled *rognon de veau* with *pommes soufflés*. And then I'd like to have *fraises des bois* with a lot of cream. Is it very shameless to be so certain and so expensive?' She smiled at him inquiringly.

'It's a virtue, and anyway it's only a good plain wholesome meal.' He turned to the *maître d'hôtel*, 'and bring plenty of toast.'

'The trouble always is,' he explained to Vesper, 'not how to get enough caviar, but how to get enough toast with it.'

'Now,' he turned back to the menu, 'I myself will accompany Mademoiselle with the caviar, but then I would like a very small *tournedos*, underdone, with *sauce Béarnaise* and a *coeur d'artichaut*. While Mademoiselle is enjoying the strawberries, I will have half an avocado pear with a little French dressing. Do you approve?'

The *maître d'hôtel* bowed.

'My compliments, mademoiselle and monsieur. Monsieur George,' he turned to the *sommelier* and repeated the two dinners for his benefit.

'*Parfait*,' said the *sommelier*, proffering the leather-bound wine list.

'If you agree,' said Bond, 'I would prefer to drink champagne with you tonight. It is a cheerful wine and it suits the occasion – I hope,' he added.

'Yes I would like champagne,' she said.

With his finger on the page, Bond turned to the *sommelier*: 'The Taittinger 45?'

'A fine wine, monsieur,' said the *sommelier*. 'But if Monsieur will permit,' he pointed with his pencil, 'the Blanc de Blanc Brut 1943 of the same marque is without equal.'

Bond smiled. 'So be it,' he said.

'That is not a well-known brand,' Bond explained to his companion, 'but it is probably the finest champagne in the world.' He grinned suddenly at the touch of pretension in his remark.

'You must forgive me,' he said. 'I take a ridiculous

pleasure in what I eat and drink. It comes partly from being a bachelor, but mostly from a habit of taking a lot of trouble over details. It's very pernickety and old-maidish really, but then when I'm working I generally have to eat my meals alone and it makes them more interesting when one takes trouble.'

Vesper smiled at him.

'I like it,' she said. 'I like doing everything fully, getting the most out of everything one does. I think that's the way to live. But it sounds rather schoolgirlish when one says it,' she added apologetically.

The little carafe of vodka had arrived in its bowl of crushed ice and Bond filled their glasses.

'Well, I agree with you anyway,' he said, 'and now, here's luck for tonight, Vesper.'

'Yes,' said the girl quietly, as she held up her small glass and looked at him with a curious directness straight in the eyes. 'I hope all will go well tonight.'

She seemed to Bond to give a quick involuntary shrug of the shoulders as she spoke, but then she leant impulsively towards him.

'I have some news for you from Mathis. He was longing to tell you himself. It's about the bomb. It's a fantastic story.'

Bond looked round, but there was no possibility of being overheard, and the caviar would be waiting for the hot toast from the kitchens.

Tell me.' His eyes glittered with interest.

'They got the third Bulgar, on the road to Paris. He was in a Citroën and he had picked up two English hikers as protective colouring. At the road-block his French was so bad that they asked for his papers and he brought out a gun and shot one of the motor-cycle patrol. But the other man got him, I don't know how, and managed to stop him committing suicide. Then they took him down to Rouen and extracted the story – in the usual French fashion, I suppose.

'Apparently they were part of a pool held in France for this sort of job – saboteurs, thugs, and so on – and Mathis's friends are already trying to round up the rest. They were to get two million francs for killing you and the agent who briefed them told them there was absolutely no chance of being caught if they followed his instructions exactly.'

She took a sip of vodka. 'But this is the interesting part.'

'The agent gave them the two camera-cases you saw.

He said the bright colours would make it easier for them. He told them that the blue case contained a very powerful smoke-bomb. The red case was the explosive. As one of them threw the red case, the other was to press a switch on the blue case and they would escape under cover of the smoke. In fact, the smoke-bomb was a pure invention to make the Bulgars think they could get away. Both cases contained an identical high-explosive bomb. There was no difference between the blue and the red cases. The idea was to destroy you and the bomb-throwers without trace. Presumably there were other plans for dealing with the third man.'

'Go on,' said Bond, full of admiration for the ingenuity of the double-cross.

'Well, apparently the Bulgars thought this sounded very fine, but cannily they decided to take no chances. It would be better, they thought, to touch off the smoke-bomb first and, from inside the cloud of smoke, hurl the explosive bomb at you. What you saw was the assistant bomb-thrower pressing down the lever on the phoney smoke-bomb and, of course, they both went up together.

'The third Bulgar was waiting behind the Splendide to pick his two friends up. When he saw what had happened, he assumed they had bungled. But the police picked up some fragments of the unexploded red bomb and he was confronted with them. When he saw that they had been tricked and that his two friends were meant to be murdered with you, he started to talk.

I expect he's still talking now. But there's nothing to link all this with Le Chiffre. They were given the job by some intermediary, perhaps one of Le Chiffre's guards, and Le Chiffre's name means absolutely nothing to the one who survived.'

She finished her story just as the waiters arrived with the caviar, a mound of hot toast, and small dishes containing finely chopped onion and grated hard-boiled egg, the white in one dish and the yolk in another.

The caviar was heaped on to their plates and they ate for a time in silence.

After a while Bond said: 'It's very satisfactory to be a corpse who changes places with his murderers. For them it certainly was a case of being hoist with their own petard. Mathis must be very pleased with the day's work – five of the opposition neutralized in twenty-four hours,' and he told her how the Muntzes had been confounded.

'Incidentally,' he asked, 'how did you come to get mixed up in this affair? What section are you in?'

'I'm personal assistant to Head of S,' said Vesper. 'As it was his plan, he wanted his section to have a hand in the operation and he asked M if I could go. It seemed only to be a liaison job, so M said yes although he told my chief that you would be furious at being given a woman to work with.' She paused and when Bond said nothing continued: 'I had to meet Mathis in Paris and come down with him. I've got a friend who is a *vend-*

euse with Dior and somehow she managed to borrow me this and the frock I was wearing this morning, otherwise I couldn't possibly have competed with all these people.' She made a gesture towards the room.

'The office was very jealous although they didn't know what the job was. All they knew was that I was to work with a Double O. Of course you're our heroes. I was enchanted.'

Bond frowned. 'It's not difficult to get a Double O number if you're prepared to kill people,' he said. 'That's all the meaning it has. It's nothing to be particularly proud of. I've got the corpses of a Japanese cipher expert in New York and a Norwegian double agent in Stockholm to thank for being a Double O. Probably quite decent people. They just got caught up in the gale of the world like that Yugoslav that Tito bumped off. It's a confusing business but if it's one's profession, one does what one's told. How do you like the grated egg with your caviar?'

'It's a wonderful combination,' she said. 'I'm loving my dinner. It seems a shame . . .' She stopped, warned by a cold look in Bond's eye.

'If it wasn't for the job, we wouldn't be here,' he said.

Suddenly he regretted the intimacy of their dinner and of their talk. He felt he had said too much and that what was only a working relationship had become confused.

'Let's consider what has to be done,' he said in a

matter-of-fact voice. 'I'd better explain what I'm going to try and do and how you can help. Which isn't very much I'm afraid,' he added.

'Now these are the basic facts.' He proceeded to sketch out the plan and enumerate the various contingencies which faced them.

The *maître d'hôtel* supervised the serving of the second course and then as they ate the delicious food, Bond continued.

She listened to him coldly, but with attentive obedience. She felt thoroughly deflated by his harshness, while admitting to herself that she should have paid more heed to the warning of Head of S.

'He's a dedicated man,' her chief had said when he gave her the assignment. 'Don't imagine this is going to be any fun. He thinks of nothing but the job on hand and, while it's on, he's absolute hell to work for. But he's an expert and there aren't many about, so you won't be wasting your time. He's a good-looking chap, but don't fall for him. I don't think he's got much heart. Anyway, good luck and don't get hurt.'

All this had been something of a challenge and she was pleased when she felt she attracted and interested him, as she knew intuitively that she did. Then at a hint that they were finding pleasure together, a hint that was only the first words of a conventional phrase, he had suddenly turned to ice and had brutally veered away as if warmth were poison to him. She felt hurt and foolish. Then she gave a mental shrug and concentrated with all her attention on what he was saying. She would not make the same mistake again.

' . . . and the main hope is to pray for a run of luck for me, or against him.'

Bond was explaining just how baccarat is played.

'It's much the same as any other gambling game. The odds against the banker and the player are more or less even. Only a run against either can be decisive and "break the bank", or break the players.

'Tonight, Le Chiffre, we know, has bought the baccarat bank from the Egyptian syndicate which is running the high tables here. He paid a million francs for it and his capital has been reduced to twenty-four million. I have about the same. There will be ten players, I expect, and we sit round the banker at a kidney-shaped table.

'Generally, this table is divided into two tableaux. The banker plays two games, one against each of the tableaux to left and right of him. In the game that banker should be able to win by playing off one tableau against the other and by first-class accountancy. But there aren't enough baccarat players yet at Royale and Le Chiffre is just going to pit his luck against the other players at the single tableau. It's unusual because the odds in favour of the banker aren't so good, but they're a shade in his favour and, of course, he has control of the size of the stakes.

'Well, the banker sits there in the middle with a croupier to rake in the cards and call the amount of each bank and a *chef de partie* to umpire the game generally. I shall be sitting as near dead opposite Le Chiffre as I can get. In front of him he has a shoe containing six packs of cards, well shuffled. There's absolutely no chance of tampering with the shoe. The cards are shuffled by the croupier and cut by one of the players and put into the shoe in full view of the table. We've checked on the staff and they're all okay. It would be useful, but almost impossible, to mark all the cards, and it would mean the connivance at least of the croupier. Anyway, we shall be watching for that too.'

Bond drank some champagne and continued.

'Now what happens at the game is this. The banker announces an opening bank of five hundred thousand francs, of five hundred pounds as it is now. Each seat is numbered from the right of the banker and the player next to the banker, or Number 1, can accept this bet and push his money out on to the table, or pass it, if it is too much for him or he doesn't want to take it. Then Number 2 has the right to take it, and if he refuses, then Number 3, and so on round the table. If no single player takes it all, the bet is offered to the table as a whole and everyone chips in, including sometimes the spectators round the table, until the five hundred thousand is made up.

'That is a small bet which would immediately be met, but when it gets to a million or two it's often difficult to find a taker or even, if the bank seems to be in luck, a group of takers to cover the bet. At the moment I shall always try and step in and accept the bet – in fact, I shall attack Le Chiffre's bank whenever I get a chance until either I've bust his bank or he's bust me. It may take some time, but in the end one of us is bound to break the other, irrespective of the other players at the table, although they can, of course, make him richer or poorer in the meantime.

'Being the banker, he's got a slight advantage in the play, but knowing that I'm making a dead set at him and not knowing, I hope, my capital, is bound to play on his nerves a bit, so I'm hoping that we start about equal.'

He paused while the strawberries came and the avocado pear.

For a while they ate in silence, then they talked of other things while the coffee was served. They smoked. Neither of them drank brandy or a liqueur. Finally, Bond felt it was time to explain the actual mechanics of the game.

'It's a simple affair,' he said, 'and you'll understand it at once if you've ever played vingt-et-un, where the object is to get cards from the banker which add up more closely to a count of twenty-one than his do. In this game, I get two cards and the banker gets two, and unless anyone wins outright, either or both of us can get one more card. The object of the game is to hold two or three cards which together count nine points, or as nearly nine as possible. Court cards and tens count nothing; aces one each; any other card its face value. It is only the last figure of your count that signifies. So nine plus seven equals six – not sixteen.

'The winner is the one whose count is nearest to nine. Draws are played over again.'

Vesper listened attentively, but she also watched the look of abstract passion on Bond's face.

'Now,' Bond continued, 'when the banker deals me my two cards, if they add up to eight or nine, they're a "natural" and I turn them up and I win, unless he has an equal or a better natural. If I haven't got a natural, I can stand on a seven or a six, perhaps ask for a card or perhaps not, on a five, and certainly ask for a card if my count is lower than five. Five is the turning point of the game. According to the odds, the chances of bettering or worsening your hand if you hold a five are exactly even.

'Only when I ask for a card or tap mine to signify that I stand on what I have, can the banker look at his. If he has a natural, he turns them up and wins. Otherwise he is faced with the same problems as I was. But he is helped in his decision to draw or not to draw a third card by my actions. If I have stood, he must assume that I have a five, six, or seven: if I have drawn, he will know that I had something less than a six and I may have improved my hand or not with the card he gave me. And this card was dealt to me face up. On its face value and a knowledge of the odds, he will know whether to take another card or to stand on his own.

'So he has a very slight advantage over me. He has a tiny help over his decision to draw or to stand. But there is always one problem card at this game – shall one draw or stand on a five and what will your opponent do with a five? Some players always draw or always stand. I follow my intuition.

'But in the end,' Bond stubbed out his cigarette and called for the bill, 'it's the natural eights and nines that matter, and I must just see that I get more of them than he does.'

While telling the story of the game and anticipating the coming fight, Bond's face had lit up again. The prospect of at least getting to grips with Le Chiffre stimulated him and quickened his pulse. He seemed to have completely forgotten the brief coolness between them, and Vesper was relieved and entered into his mood.

He paid the bill and gave a handsome tip to the *sommelier*. Vesper rose and led the way out of the restaurant and out on to the steps of the hotel.

The big Bentley was waiting and Bond drove Vesper over, parking as close to the entrance as he could. As they walked through the ornate ante-rooms, he hardly spoke. She looked at him and saw that his nostrils were slightly flared. In other respects he seemed completely at ease, acknowledging cheerfully the greetings of the Casino functionaries. At the door to the *salle privée* they were not asked for their membership cards. Bond's high gambling had already made him a favoured client and any companion of his shared in the glory.

Before they had penetrated very far into the main room, Felix Leiter detached himself from one of the roulette tables and greeted Bond as an old friend. After being introduced to Vesper Lynd and exchanging a few remarks, Leiter said: 'Well, since you're playing baccarat this evening, will you allow me to show Miss Lynd how to break the bank at roulette? I've got three lucky numbers that are bound to show soon, and I expect Miss Lynd has some too. Then perhaps we could come and watch you when your game starts to warm up.'

Bond looked inquiringly at Vesper.

'I should love that,' she said, 'but will you give me one of your lucky numbers to play on?'

'I have no lucky numbers,' said Bond unsmilingly. 'I only bet on even chances, or as near them as I can get. Well, I shall leave you then.' He excused himself. 'You will be in excellent hands with my friend Felix Leiter.' He gave a short smile which embraced them both and walked with an unhurried gait towards the *caisse*.

Leiter sensed the rebuff.

'He's a very serious gambler, Miss Lynd,' he said. 'And I guess he has to be. Now come with me and watch Number 17 obey my extra-sensory perceptions. You'll find it quite a painless sensation being given plenty of money for nothing.'

Bond was relieved to be on his own again and to be able to clear his mind of everything but the task on hand. He stood at the *caisse* and took his twenty-four million francs against the receipt which had been given him that afternoon. He divided the notes into equal packets and put half the sum into his right-hand coat pocket and the other half into the left. Then he strolled slowly across the room between the thronged tables until he came to the top of the room where the broad baccarat table waited behind the brass rail.

The table was filling up and the cards were spread face down being stirred and mixed slowly in what is known as the 'croupiers' shuffle', supposedly the shuffle which is most effective and least susceptible to cheating.

The *chef de partie* lifted the velvet-covered chain which allowed entrance through the brass rail.

'I've kept Number 6 as you wished, Monsieur Bond.'

There were still three other empty places at the table. Bond moved inside the rail to where a *huissier* was holding out his chair. He sat down with a nod to the players on his right and left. He took out his wide gunmetal cigarette-case and his black lighter and placed them on the green baize at his right elbow. The *huissier* wiped a thick glass ash-tray with a cloth and put it beside them. Bond lit a cigarette and leant back in his chair.

Opposite him, the banker's chair was vacant. He glanced round the table. He knew most of the players by sight, but few of their names. At Number 7, on his right, there was a Monsieur Sixte, a wealthy Belgian with metal interests in the Congo. At Number 9 there was Lord Danvers, a distinguished but weak-looking man whose francs were presumably provided by his rich American wife, a middle-aged woman with the predatory mouth of a barracuda, who sat at Number 3. Bond reflected that they would probably play a pawky and nervous game and be amongst the early casualties. At Number 1, to the right of the bank was a well-known Greek gambler who owned, as in Bond's experience apparently everyone does in the Eastern Mediterranean, a profitable shipping line. He would play coldly and well and would be a stayer.

Bond asked the *huissier* for a card and wrote on it, under a neat question mark, the remaining numbers, 2, 4, 5, 8, 10, and asked the *huissier* to give it to the *chef de partie*.

Soon it came back with the names filled in.

Number 2, still empty, was to be Carmel Delane, the American film star with alimony from three husbands to burn and, Bond assumed, a call on still more from whoever her present companion at Royale might be. With her sanguine temperament she would play gaily and with panache and might run into a vein of luck.

Then came Lady Danvers at Number 3 and Numbers 4 and 5 were a Mr and Mrs Du Pont, rich-looking and might or might not have some of the real Du Pont money behind them. Bond guessed they would be stayers. They both had a business-like look about them and were talking together easily and cheerfully as if they felt very much at home at the big game. Bond was quite happy to have them next to him – Mrs Du Pont sat at Number 5 – and he felt prepared to share with them or with Monsieur Sixte on his right, if they found themselves faced with too big a bank.

At Number 8 was the Maharajah of a small Indian state, probably with all his wartime sterling balances to play with. Bond's experience told him that few of the Asiatic races were courageous gamblers, even the much-vaunted Chinese being inclined to lose heart if the going was bad. But the Maharajah would probably stay in the game and stand some heavy losses if they were gradual.

Number 10 was a prosperous-looking young Italian, Signor Tomelli, who possibly had plenty of money from rackrents in Milan and would probably play a dashing and foolish game. He might lose his temper and make a scene.

Bond had just finished his sketchy summing-up of the players when Le Chiffre, with the silence and economy of movement of a big fish, came through the opening in the brass rail and, with a cold smile of welcome for the table, took his place directly opposite Bond in the banker's chair.

With the same economy of movement, he cut the thick slab of cards which the croupier had placed on the table squarely between his blunt relaxed hands. Then, as the croupier fitted the six packs with one swift exact motion into the metal and wooden shoe, Le Chiffre said something quietly to him.

'*Messieurs, mesdames, les jeux sont faits. Un banco de cinq cent mille,*' and as the Greek at Number 1 tapped the table in front of his fat pile of hundred-mille plaques, 'Le banco est fait.'

Le Chiffre crouched over the shoe. He gave it a short deliberate slap to settle the cards, the first of which showed its semicircular pale pink tongue through the slanting aluminium mouth of the shoe. Then, with a thick white fore-finger he pressed gently on the pink tongue and slipped out the first card six inches or a foot towards the Greek on his right hand. Then he slipped out a card for himself, then another for the Greek, then one more for himself.

He sat immobile, not touching his own cards.

He looked at the Greek's face.

With his flat wooden spatula, like a long bricklayer's trowel, the croupier delicately lifted up the Greek's two cards and dropped them with a quick movement an extra few inches to the right so that they lay just before the Greek's pale hairy hands which lay inert like two watchful pink crabs on the table.

The two pink crabs scuttled out together and the Greek gathered the cards into his wide left hand and cautiously bent his head so that he could see, in the shadow made by his cupped hand, the value of the bottom of the two cards. Then he slowly inserted the forefinger of his right hand and slipped the bottom card slightly sideways so that the value of the top card was also just perceptible.

His face was quite impassive. He flattened out his left hand on the table and then withdrew it, leaving the two pink cards face down before him, their secret unrevealed.

Then he lifted his head and looked Le Chiffre in the eye.

'*Non*,' said the Greek flatly.

From the decision to stand on his two cards and not ask for another, it was clear that the Greek had a five, or a six, or a seven. To be certain of winning, the banker had to reveal an eight or a nine. If the banker failed to show either figure, he also had the right to take another card which might or might not improve his count.

Le Chiffre's hands were clasped in front of him, his two cards three or four inches away. With his right hand he picked up the two cards and turned them face upwards on the table with a faint snap.

They were a four and a five, an undefeatable natural nine.

He had won.

'*Neuf à la banque*,' quietly said the croupier. With his spatula he faced the Greek's two cards, '*Et le sept*,' he said unemotionally, lifting up gently the corpses of the seven and queen and slipping them through the wide slot in the table near his chair which leads into the gib metal canister to which all dead cards are consigned. Le Chiffre's two cards followed them with a faint rattle which comes from the canister at the beginning of each session before the discards have made a cushion over the metal floor of their oubliette.

The Greek pushed forward five plaques of one

hundred thousand and the croupier added these to Le Chiffre's half-million plaque which lay in the centre of the table. From each bet the Casino takes a tiny percentage, the *cagnotte*, but it is usual at a big game for the banker to subscribe this himself either in a prearranged lump or by contributions at the end of each hand, so that the amount of the bank's stake can always be a round figure. Le Chiffre had chosen the second course.

The croupier slipped some counters through the slot in the table which receives the *cagnotte* and announced quietly:

'*Un banco d'un million.*'

'*Suivi,*' murmured the Greek, meaning that he exercised his right to follow up his lost bet.

Bond lit a cigarette and settled himself in his chair. The long game was launched and the sequence of these gestures and the reiteration of this subdued litany would continue until the end came and the players dispersed. Then the enigmatic cards would be burnt or defaced, a shroud would be draped over the table and the grass-green baize battlefield would soak up the blood of its victims and refresh itself.

The Greek, after taking a third card, could achieve no better than a four to the bank's seven.

'*Un banco de deux millions,*' said the croupier.

The players on Bond's left remained silent.

'*Banco,*' said Bond.

Le Chiffre looked incuriously at him, the whites of his eyes, which showed all round the irises, lending something impassive and doll-like to his gaze.

He slowly removed one thick hand from the table and slipped it into the pocket of his dinner-jacket. The hand came out holding a small metal cylinder with a cap which Le Chiffre unscrewed. He inserted the nozzle of the cylinder, with an obscene deliberation, twice into each black nostril in turn, and luxuriously inhaled the benzedrine vapour.

Unhurriedly he pocketed the inhaler, then his hand came quickly back above the level of the table and gave the shoe its usual hard, sharp slap.

During this offensive pantomime Bond had coldly held the banker's gaze, taking in the wide expanse of white face surmounted by the short abrupt cliff of reddish-brown hair, the unsmiling wet red mouth and the impressive width of the shoulders, loosely draped in a massively cut dinner-jacket.

But for the high-lights on the satin of the shawl-cut lapels, he might have been faced by the thick bust of a black-fleeced Minotaur rising out of a green grass field.

Bond slipped a packet of notes on to the table without

counting them. If he lost, the croupier would extract what was necessary to cover the bet, but the easy gesture conveyed that Bond didn't expect to lose and that this was only a token display from the deep funds at Bond's disposal.

The other players sensed a tension between the two gamblers and there was silence as Le Chiffre fingered the four cards out of the shoe.

The croupier slipped Bond's two cards across to him with the tip of his spatula. Bond, still with his eyes holding Le Chiffre's, reached his right hand out a few inches, glanced down very swiftly, then as he looked up again impassively at Le Chiffre, with a disdainful gesture he tossed the cards face upwards on the table.

They were a four and a five – an unbeatable nine.

There was a little gasp of envy from the table and the players to the left of Bond exchanged rueful glances at their failure to accept the two million franc bet.

With a hint of a shrug, Le Chiffre slowly faced his own two cards and flicked them away with his fingernail. They were two valueless knaves.

'*Le baccarat*,' intoned the croupier as he spaded the thick chips over the table to Bond.

Bond slipped them into his right-hand pocket with the unused packet of notes. His face showed no emotion, but he was pleased with the success of his first coup and with the outcome of the silent clash of wills across the table.

The woman on his left, the American Mrs Du Pont, turned to him with a wry smile.

'I shouldn't have let it come to you,' she said. 'Directly the cards were dealt I kicked myself.'

'It's only the beginning of the game,' said Bond. 'You may be right the next time you pass it.'

Mr Du Pont leant forward from the other side of his wife: 'If one could be right every hand, none of us would be here,' he said philosophically.

'I would be,' his wife laughed. 'You don't think I do this for pleasure.'

As the game went on, Bond looked over the spectators leaning on the high brass rail round the table. He soon saw Le Chiffre's two gunmen. They stood behind and to either side of the banker. They looked respectable enough, but not sufficiently a part of the game to be unobtrusive.

The one more or less behind Le Chiffre's right arm was tall and funereal in his dinner-jacket. His face was wooden and grey, but his eyes flickered and gleamed like a conjurer's. His whole long body was restless and his hands shifted often on the brass rail. Bond guessed that he would kill without interest or concern for what he killed and that he would prefer strangling. He had something of Lennie in *Of Mice and Men*, but his inhumanity would not come from infantilism but from drugs. Marihuana, decided Bond.

The other man looked like a Corsican shopkeeper. He was short and very dark with a flat head covered with thickly greased hair. He seemed to be a cripple. A chunky malacca cane with a rubber tip hung on the rail beside him. He must have had permission to bring the cane into the Casino with him, reflected Bond, who knew that neither sticks nor any other objects were allowed in the rooms as a precaution against acts of violence. He looked sleek and well fed. His mouth hung vacantly half-open and revealed very bad teeth. He wore a heavy black moustache and the backs of his hands on the rail were matted with black hair. Bond guessed that hair covered most of his squat body. Naked, Bond supposed, he would be an obscene object.

The game continued uneventfully, but with a slight bias against the bank.

The third coup is the 'sound barrier' at chemin-de-fer and baccarat. Your luck can defeat the first and second tests, but when the third deal comes along it most often spells disaster. Again and again at this point you find yourself being bounced back to earth. It was like that now. Neither the bank nor any of the players seemed to be able to get hot. But there was a steady and inexorable seepage against the bank, amounting after about two hours' play to ten million francs. Bond had no idea what profits Le Chiffre had made over the past two days. He estimated them at five million and guessed that now the banker's capital could not be more than twenty million.

In fact, Le Chiffre had lost heavily all that afternoon. At this moment he only had ten million left.

Bond, on the other hand, by one o'clock in the morning, had won four million, bringing his resources up to twenty-eight million.

Bond was cautiously pleased. Le Chiffre showed no trace of emotion. He continued to play like an automaton, never speaking except when he gave instructions in a low aside to the croupier at the opening of each new bank.

Outside the pool of silence round the high table, there was the constant hum of the other tables, chemin-de-fer, roulette and trente-et-quarante, interspersed with the clear calls of the croupiers and occasional bursts of laughter or gasps of excitement from different corners of the huge *salle*.

In the background there thudded always the hidden metronome of the Casino, ticking up its little treasure of one-per-cents with each spin of a wheel and each turn of a card – a pulsing fat-cat with a zero for a heart.

It was at ten minutes past one by Bond's watch when, at the high table, the whole pattern of play suddenly altered.

The Greek at Number I was still having a bad time. He had lost the first coup of half a million francs and the second. He passed the third time, leaving a bank of two millions. Carmel Delane at Number 2 refused it. So did Lady Danvers at Number 3.

The Du Ponts looked at each other.

'*Banco*,' said Mrs Du Pont, and promptly lost to the banker's natural eight.

'*Un banco de quatre millions*,' said the croupier.

'*Banco*,' said Bond, pushing out a wad of notes.

Again he fixed Le Chiffre with his eye. Again he gave only a cursory look at his two cards.

'No,' he said. He held a marginal five. The position was dangerous.

Le Chiffre turned up a knave and a four. He gave the shoe another slap. He drew a three.

'*Sept à la banque*', said the croupier, '*et cinq*,' he added as he tipped Bond's losing cards face upwards. He raked over Bond's money, extracted four million francs and returned the remainder to Bond.

'*Un banco de huit millions*.'

'*Suivi*,' said Bond.

And lost again, to a natural nine.

In two coups he had lost twelve million francs. By scraping the barrel, he had just sixteen million francs left, exactly the amount of the next banco.

Suddenly Bond felt the sweat on his palms. Like snow in sunshine his capital had melted. With the covetous deliberation of the winning gambler, Le Chiffre was tapping a light tattoo on the table with his right hand. Bond looked across into the eyes of murky basalt. They held an ironical question. 'Do you want the full treatment?' they seemed to ask.

'*Suivi*,' Bond said softly.

He took some notes and plaques out of his right-hand pocket and the entire stack of notes out of his left and pushed them forward. There was no hint in his movements that this would be his last stake.

His mouth felt suddenly as dry as flock wall-paper. He looked up and saw Vesper and Felix Leiter standing where the gunman with the stick had stood. He did not know how long they had been standing there. Leiter looked faintly worried, but Vesper smiled encouragement at him.

He heard a faint rattle on the rail behind him and turned his head. The battery of bad teeth under the black moustache gaped vacantly back at him.

'*Le jeu est fait*,' said the croupier, and the two cards came slithering towards him over the green baize – a green baize which was no longer smooth, but thick now, and furry and almost choking, its colour as livid as the grass on a fresh tomb.

The light from the broad satin-lined shades which had seemed so welcoming now seemed to take the colour out of his hand as he glanced at the cards. Then he looked again.

It was nearly as bad as it could have been – the king of hearts and an ace, the ace of spades. It squinted up at him like a black widow spider.

'A card.' He still kept all emotion out of his voice.

Le Chiffre faced his own two cards. He had a queen and a black five. He looked at Bond and pressed out another card with a wide forefinger. The table was absolutely silent. He faced it and flicked it away. The croupier lifted it delicately with his spatula and slipped it over to Bond. It was a good card, the five of hearts, but to Bond it was a difficult fingerprint in dried blood. He now had a count of six and Le Chiffre a count of five, but the banker, having a five and giving a five, would and must draw another card and try and improve with a one, two, three or four. Drawing any other card he would be defeated.

The odds were on Bond's side, but now it was Le Chiffre who looked across into Bond's eyes and hardly glanced at the card as he flicked it face upwards on the table.

It was, unnecessarily, the best, a four, giving the bank a count of nine. He had won, almost slowing up.

Bond was beaten and cleaned out.

Bond sat silent, frozen with defeat. He opened his wide black case and took out a cigarette. He snapped open the tiny jaws of the Ronson and lit the cigarette and put the lighter back on the table. He took a deep lungful of smoke and expelled it between his teeth with a faint hiss.

What now? Back to the hotel and bed, avoiding the commiserating eyes of Mathis and Leiter and Vesper. Back to the telephone call to London, and then tomorrow the plane home, the taxi up to Regent's Park, the walk up the stairs and along the corridor, and M's cold face across the table, his forced sympathy, his 'better luck next time' and, of course, there couldn't be one, not another chance like this.

He looked round the table and up at the spectators. Few were looking at him. They were waiting while the croupier counted the money and piled up the chips in a neat stack in front of the banker, waiting to see if anyone would conceivably challenge this huge bank of thirty-two million francs, this wonderful run of banker's luck.

Leiter had vanished, not wishing to look Bond in the

eye after the knock-out, he supposed. Yet Vesper looked curiously unmoved, she gave him a smile of encouragement. But then, Bond reflected, she knew nothing of the game. Had no notion, probably, of the bitterness of his defeat.

The *huissier* was coming towards Bond inside the rail. He stopped beside him. Bent over him. Placed a squat envelope beside Bond on the table. It was as thick as a dictionary. Said something about the *caisse*. Moved away again.

Bond's heart thumped. He took the heavy anonymous envelope below the level of the table and slit it open with his thumbnail, noticing that the gum was still wet on the flap.

Unbelieving and yet knowing it was true, he felt the broad wads of notes. He slipped them into his pockets, retaining the half-sheet of note-paper which was pinned to the topmost of them. He glanced at it in the shadow below the table. There was one line of writing in ink: 'Marshall Aid. Thirty-two million francs. With the compliments of the USA.'

Bond swallowed. He looked over towards Vesper. Felix Leiter was again standing beside her. He grinned slightly and Bond smiled back and raised his hand from the table in a small gesture of benediction. Then he set his mind to sweeping away all traces of the sense of complete defeat which had swamped him a few minutes before. This was a reprieve, but only a reprieve. There could be no more miracles. This time he had to win – if Le Chiffre had not already made his fifty million – if he was going to go on!

The croupier had completed his task of computing the *cagnotte*, changing Bond's notes into plaques and making a pile of the giant stake in the middle of the table.

There lay thirty-two thousand pounds. Perhaps, thought Bond, Le Chiffre needed just one more coup, even a minor one of a few million francs, to achieve his object. Then he would have made his fifty million francs and would leave the table. By tomorrow his deficits would be covered and his position secure.

He showed no signs of moving and Bond guessed with relief that somehow he must have overestimated Le Chiffre's resources.

The then only hope, thought Bond, was to stamp on him now. Not to share the bank with the table, or to take some minor part of it, but to go the whole hog. This would really jolt Le Chiffre. He would hate to see more than ten or fifteen million of the stake covered, and he could not possibly expect anyone to banco the entire thirty-two millions. He might not know that Bond had been cleaned out, but he must imagine that Bond had by now only small reserves. He could not know of the contents of the envelope; if he did, he would probably withdraw the bank and start all over again on the wearisome journey up from the five hundred thousand franc opening bet.

The analysis was right.

Le Chiffre needed another eight million.

At last he nodded.

'*Un banco de trente-deux millions.*'

The croupier's voice rang out. A silence built itself up round the table.

'*Un banco de trente-deux millions.*'

In a louder, prouder voice the *chef de partie* took up the cry, hoping to draw big money away from the neighbouring chemin-de-fer tables. Besides, this was wonderful publicity. The stake had only once been reached in the history of baccarat – at Deauville in 1950. The rival Casino de la Forêt at Le Touquet had never got near it.

It was then that Bond leant slightly forward.

'*Suivi,*' he said quietly.

There was an excited buzz round the table. The word ran through the Casino. People crowded in. Thirty-two million! For most of them it was more than they had earned all their lives. It was their savings and the savings of their families. It was, literally, a small fortune.

One of the Casino directors consulted with the *chef de partie*. The *chef de partie* turned apologetically to Bond.

'*Excusez moi, monsieur. La mise?*'

It was an indication that Bond really must show he had the money to cover the bet. They knew, of course, that he was a very wealthy man, but after all, thirty-two millions! And it sometimes happened that desperate people would bet without a sou in the world and cheerfully go to prison if they lost.

'*Mes excuses, Monsieur Bond*,' added the *chef de partie* obsequiously.

It was when Bond shovelled the great wad of notes out on to the table and the croupier busied himself with the task of counting the pinned sheaves of ten thousand franc notes, the largest denomination issued in France, that he caught a swift exchange of glances between Le Chiffre and the gunman standing directly behind Bond.

Immediately he felt something hard press into the base of his spine, right into the cleft between his two buttocks on the padded chair.

At the same time a thick voice speaking southern French said softly, urgently, just behind his right ear:

'This is a gun, monsieur. It is absolutely silent. It can blow the base of your spine off without a sound. You will appear to have fainted. I shall be gone. Withdraw your bet before I count ten. If you call for help I shall fire.'

The voice was confident. Bond believed it. These people had shown they would unhesitatingly go the limit. The thick walking-stick was explained. Bond knew the type of gun. The barrel a series of soft rubber baffles which absorbed the detonation, but allowed the passage of the bullet. They had been invented and used in the war for assassinations. Bond had tested them himself.

'*Un*,' said the voice.

Bond turned his head. There was the man, leaning forward close behind him, smiling broadly under his black moustache as if he was wishing Bond luck, completely secure in the noise and the crowd.

The discoloured teeth came together. '*Deux*,' said the grinning mouth.

Bond looked across. Le Chiffre was watching him. His eyes glittered back at Bond. His mouth was open and he was breathing fast. He was waiting, waiting for Bond's hand to gesture to the croupier, or else for Bond suddenly to slump backwards in his chair, his face grimacing with a scream.

'*Trois*.'

Bond looked over at Vesper and Felix Leiter. They were smiling and talking to each other. The fools. Where was Mathis? Where were those famous men of his?

'*Quatre*.'

And the other spectators. This crowd of jabbering idiots. Couldn't someone see what was happening? The *chef de partie*, the croupier, the *huissier*?

'*Cinq*.'

The croupier was tidying up the pile of notes. The *chef de partie* bowed smilingly towards Bond. Directly the stake was in order he would announce: '*Le jeux est fait*', and the gun would fire whether the gunman had reached ten or not.

'*Six*.'

Bond decided. It was a chance. He carefully moved his hands to the edge of the table, gripped it, edged his buttocks right back, feeling the sharp gun-sight grind into his coccyx.

'*Sept.*'

The *chef de partie* turned to Le Chiffre with his eyebrows lifted, waiting for the banker's nod that he was ready to play.

Suddenly Bond heaved backwards with all his strength. His momentum tipped the cross-bar of the chair-back down so quickly that it cracked across the malacca tube and wrenched it from the gunman's hand before he could pull the trigger.

Bond went head-over-heels on to the ground amongst the spectators' feet, his legs in the air. The back of the chair splintered with a sharp crack. There were cries of dismay. The spectators cringed away and then, reassured, clustered back. Hands helped him to his feet and brushed him down. The *huissier* bustled up with the *chef de partie*. At all costs a scandal must be avoided.

Bond held on to the brass rail. He looked confused and embarrassed. He brushed his hands across his forehead.

'A momentary faintness,' he said. 'It is nothing – the excitement, the heat.'

There were expressions of sympathy. Naturally, with this tremendous game. Would Monsieur prefer to withdraw, to lie down, to go home? Should a doctor be fetched?

Bond shook his head. He was perfectly all right now. His excuses to the table. To the banker also.

A new chair was brought and he sat down. He looked across at Le Chiffre. Through his relief at being alive, he felt a moment of triumph at what he saw – some fear in the fat, pale face.

There was a buzz of speculation round the table. Bond's neighbours on both sides of him bent forward and spoke solicitously about the heat and the lateness of the hour and the smoke and the lack of air.

Bond replied politely. He turned to examine the crowd behind him. There was no trace of the gunman, but the *huissier* was looking for someone to claim the malacca stick. It seemed undamaged. But it no longer carried a rubber tip. Bond beckoned to him.

'If you will give it to that gentleman over there,' he indicated Felix Leiter, 'he will return it. It belongs to an acquaintance of his.'

The *hussier* bowed.

Bond grimly reflected that a short examination would reveal to Leiter why he had made such an embarrassing public display of himself.

He turned back to the table and tapped the green cloth in front of him to show that he was ready.

13 / 'A WHISPER OF LOVE, A WHISPER OF HATE'

'*La partie continue*,' announced the *chef* impressively. '*Un banco de trente-deux millions.*'

The spectators craned forward. Le Chiffre hit the shoe with a flat-handed slap that made it rattle. As an afterthought he took out his benzedrine inhaler and sucked the vapour up his nose.

'Filthy brute,' said Mrs Du Pont on Bond's left.

Bond's mind was clear again. By a miracle he had survived a devastating wound. He could feel his armpits still wet with the fear of it. But the success of his gambit with the chair had wiped out all memories of the dreadful valley of defeat through which he had just passed.

He had made a fool of himself. The game had been interrupted for at least ten minutes, a delay unheard of in a respectable casino, but now the cards were waiting for him in the shoe. They must not fail him. He felt his heart lift at the prospect of what was to come.

It was two o'clock in the morning. Apart from the thick crowd round the big game, play was still going on at three of the chemin-de-fer games and at the same number of roulette tables.

In the silence round his own table, Bond suddenly heard a distant croupier intone: '*Neuf. Le rouge gagne, impair et manque.*'

Was this an omen for him or for Le Chiffre?

The two cards slithered towards him across the green sea.

Like an octopus under a rock, Le Chiffre watched him from the other side of the table.

Bond reached out a steady right hand and drew the cards towards him. Would it be the lift of the heart which a nine brings, or an eight brings?

He fanned the two cards under the curtain of his hand. The muscles of his jaw rippled as he clenched his teeth. His whole body stiffened in a reflex of self-defence.

He had two queens, two red queens.

They looked roguishly back at him from the shadows. They were the worst. They were nothing. Zero. Baccarat.

'A card,' said Bond fighting to keep hopelessness out of his voice. He felt Le Chiffre's eyes boring into his brain.

The banker slowly turned his own two cards face up.

He had a count of three – a king and a black three.

Bond softly exhaled a cloud of tobacco smoke. He still had a chance. Now he was really faced with the moment of truth. Le Chiffre slapped the shoe, slipped out a card, Bond's fate, and slowly turned it face up.

It was a nine, a wonderful nine of hearts, the card known in gipsy magic as 'a whisper of love, a whisper of hate', the card that meant almost certain victory for Bond.

The croupier slipped it delicately across. To Le Chiffre it meant nothing. Bond might have had a one, in which case he now had ten points, or nothing, or baccarat, as it is called. Or he might have had a two, three, four, or even five. In which case, with the nine, his maximum count would be four.

Holding a three and giving nine is one of the moot situations at the game. The odds are so nearly divided between to draw or not to draw. Bond let the banker sweat it out. Since his nine could only be equalled by the banker drawing a six, he would normally have shown his count if it had been a friendly game.

Bond's cards lay on the table before him, the two impersonal pale pink-patterned backs and the faced nine of hearts. To Le Chiffre the nine might be telling the truth or many variations of lies.

The whole secret lay in the reverse of the two pink backs where the pair of queens kissed the green cloth.

The sweat was running down either side of the banker's beaky nose. His thick tongue came out slyly and licked a drop out of the corner of his red gash of a mouth. He looked at Bond's cards, and then at his own, and then back at Bond's.

Then his whole body shrugged and he slipped out a card for himself from the lisping shoe.

He faced it. The table craned. It was a wonderful card, a five.

'*Huit à la banque*,' said the croupier.

As Bond sat silent, Le Chiffre suddenly grinned wolfishly. He must have won.

The croupier's spatula reached almost apologetically across the table. There was not a man at the table who did not believe Bond was defeated.

The spatula flicked the two pink cards over on their backs. The gay red queens smiled up at the lights.

'*Et le neuf.*'

A great gasp went up round the table, and then a hubbub of talk.

Bond's eyes were on Le Chiffre. The big man fell back in his chair as if slugged above the heart. His mouth opened and shut once or twice in protest and his right hand felt at his throat. Then he rocked back. His lips were grey.

As the huge stack of plaques was shunted across the table to Bond the banker reached into an inner pocket of his jacket and threw a wad of notes on to the table.

The croupier riffled through them.

'*Un banco de dix millions*,' he announced. He slapped down their equivalent in ten plaques of a million each.

This is the kill, thought Bond. This man has reached the point of no return. This is the last of his capital. He has come to where I stood an hour ago and he is making the last gesture that I made. But if this man loses, there is no one to come to his aid, no miracle to help him.

Bond sat back and lit a cigarette. On a small table beside him half a bottle of Clicquot and a glass had materialized. Without asking who the benefactor was, Bond filled the glass to the brim and drank it down in two long draughts.

Then he leant back with his arms curled forward on the table in front of him like the arms of a wrestler seeking a hold at the opening of a bout of ju-jitsu.

The players on his left remained silent.

'*Banco,*' he said, speaking straight at Le Chiffre.

Once more the two cards were borne over to him and this time the croupier slipped them into the green lagoon between the outstretched arms.

Bond curled his right hand in, glanced briefly down and flipped the cards face up into the middle of the table.

'*Le Neuf,*' said the croupier.

Le Chiffre was gazing down at his own two black kings.

'*Et le baccarat,*' and the croupier eased across the table the fat tide of plaques.

Le Chiffre watched them go to join the serried millions in the shadow of Bond's left arm, then he stood up slowly and without a word he brushed past the players to the break in the rail. He unhooked the velvet-covered chain and let it fall. The spectators opened a way for him. They looked at him curiously and rather fearfully as if he carried the smell of death on him. Then he vanished from Bond's sight.

Bond stood up. He took a hundred-mille plaque from the stacks beside him and slipped it across the table to the *chef de partie*. He cut short the effusive thanks and asked the croupier to have his winnings carried to the *caisse*. The other players were leaving their seats. With no banker, there could be no game, and by now it was half past two. He exchanged some pleasant words with his neighbours to right and left and then ducked under the rail to where Vesper and Felix Leiter were waiting for him.

Together they walked over to the *caisse*. Bond was invited to come into the private office of the Casino directors. On the desk lay his huge pile of chips. He added the contents of his pockets to it.

In all there was over seventy million francs.

Bond took Felix Leiter's money in notes and took a cheque to cash on the Crédit Lyonnais for the remaining forty-odd million. He was congratulated warmly on his winnings. The directors hoped that he would be playing again that evening.

Bond gave an evasive reply. He walked over to the bar and handed Leiter's money to him. For a few minutes they discussed the game over a bottle of champagne. Leiter took a .45 bullet out of his pocket and placed it on the table.

'I gave the gun to Mathis,' he said. 'He's taken it away. He was as puzzled as we were by the spill you took. He was standing at the back of the crowd with one of his men when it happened. The gunman got away without difficulty. You can imagine how they kicked themselves when they saw the gun. Mathis gave me this bullet to show you what you escaped. The nose has been cut with a dumdum cross. You'd have been in a terrible mess. But they can't tie it on to Le Chiffre. The man came in alone. They've got the form he filled up to get his entrance card. Of course, it'll all be phony. He got permission to bring the stick in with him. He had a certificate for a war-wound pension. These people certainly get them-selves well organized. They've got his prints and they're on the Belinograph to Paris, so we may hear more about him in the morning.' Felix Leiter tapped out another cigarette. 'Anyway, all's well that ends well. You certainly took Le Chiffre for a ride at the end, though we had some bad moments. I expect you did too.'

Bond smiled. 'That envelope was the most won-derful thing that ever happened to me. I thought I was really finished. It wasn't at all a pleasant feeling. Talk about a friend in need. One day I'll try and return the compliment.'

He rose. 'I'll just go over to the hotel and put this away,' he said, tapping his pocket. 'I don't like wan-dering around with Le Chiffre's death-warrant on me. He might get ideas. Then I'd like to celebrate a bit. What do you think?'

He turned to Vesper. She had hardly said a word since the end of the game.

'Shall we have a glass of champagne in the night-club before we go to bed? It's called the Roi Galant. You get to it through the public rooms. It looks quite cheerful.'

'I think I'd love to,' said Vesper. 'I'll tidy up while you put your winnings away. I'll meet you in the entrance hall.'

'What about you, Felix?' Bond hoped he could be alone with Vesper.

Leiter looked at him and read his mind.

'I'd rather take a little rest before breakfast,' he said. 'It's been quite a day and I expect Paris will want me to do a bit of mopping-up tomorrow. There are several loose ends you won't have to worry about. I shall. I'll walk over to the hotel with you. Might as well convoy the treasure ship right into port.'

They strolled over through the shadows cast by the full moon. Both had their hands on their guns. It was three o'clock in the morning, but there were several people about and the courtyard of the Casino was still lined with motorcars.

The short walk was uneventful.

At the hotel, Leiter insisted on accompanying Bond to his room. It was as Bond had left it six hours before.

'No reception committee,' observed Leiter, 'but I wouldn't put it past them to try a last throw. Do you think I ought to stay up and keep you two company?'

'You get your sleep,' said Bond. 'Don't worry about us. They won't be interested in me without the money and I've got an idea for looking after that. Thanks for all you've done. I hope we get on a job again one day.'

'Suits me,' said Leiter, 'so long as you can draw a nine when it's needed – and bring Vesper along with you,' he added dryly. He went out and closed the door.

Bond turned back to the friendliness of his room.

After the crowded arena of the big table and the nervous strain of the three hours' play, he was glad to be alone for a moment and be welcomed by his pyjamas on the bed and his hairbrushes on the dressing-table. He went into the bathroom and dashed cold water over his face and gargled with a sharp mouthwash. He felt the bruises on the back of his head and on his right shoulder. He reflected cheerfully how narrowly he had twice that day escaped being murdered. Would he have to sit up all that night and wait for them to come again, or was Le Chiffre even now on his way to Le Havre or Bordeaux to pick up a boat for some corner of the world where he could escape the eyes and the guns of SMERSH?

Bond shrugged his shoulders. Sufficient unto that day had been its evil. He gazed for a moment into the mirror and wondered about Vesper's morals. He wanted her cold and arrogant body. He wanted to see tears and desire in her remote blue eyes and to take the ropes of her black hair in his hands and bend her long body back under his. Bond's eyes narrowed and his face in the mirror looked back at him with hunger.

He turned away and took out of his pocket the cheque for forty million francs. He folded this very small. Then he opened the door and looked up and down the corridor. He left the door wide open and with his ears cocked for footsteps or the sound of the lift, he set to work with a small screwdriver.

Five minutes later he gave a last-minute survey to his handiwork, put some fresh cigarettes in his case, closed and locked the door and went off down the corridor and across the hall and out into the moonlight.

The entrance to the Roi Galant was a seven-foot golden picture-frame which had once, perhaps, enclosed the vast portrait of a noble European. It was in a discreet corner of the 'kitchen' – the public roulette and boule room, where several tables were still busy. As Bond took Vesper's arm and led her over the gilded step, he fought back a hankering to borrow some money from the *caisse* and plaster maximums over the nearest table. But he knew that this would be a brash and cheap gesture *pour épater la bourgeoisie*. Whether he won or lost, it would be a kick in the teeth to the luck which had been given him.

The night-club was small and dark, lit only by candles in gilded candelabra whose warm light was repeated in wall mirrors set in more gold picture-frames. The walls were covered in dark red satin and the chairs and *banquettes* in matching red plush. In the far corner, a trio, consisting of a piano, an electric guitar and drums, was playing 'La Vie en Rose' with muted sweetness. Seduction dripped on the quietly throbbing air. It seemed to Bond that every couple must be touching with passion under the tables.

They were given a corner table near the door. Bond

ordered a bottle of Veuve Clicquot and scrambled eggs and bacon.

They sat for a time listening to the music and then Bond turned to Vesper: 'It's wonderful sitting here with you and knowing the job's finished. It's a lovely end to the day – the prize-giving.'

He expected her to smile. She said: 'Yes, isn't it,' in a rather brittle voice. She seemed to be listening carefully to the music. One elbow rested on the table and her hand supported her chin, but on the back of her hand and not on the palm, and Bond noticed that her knuckles showed white as if her fist was tightly clenched.

Between the thumb and first two fingers of her right hand she held one of Bond's cigarettes, as an artist holds a crayon, and though she smoked with composure, she tapped the cigarette occasionally into an ash-try when the cigarette had no ash.

Bond noticed these small things because he felt intensely aware of her and because he wanted to draw her into his own feeling of warmth and relaxed sensuality. But he accepted her reserve. He thought it came from a desire to protect herself from him, or else it was her reaction to his coolness to her earlier in the evening, his deliberate coolness, which he knew had been taken as a rebuff.

He was patient. He drank champagne and talked a little about the happenings of the day and about the personalities of Mathis and Leiter and about the possible consequences for Le Chiffre. He was discreet and he only talked about the aspects of the case on which she must have been briefed by London.

She answered perfunctorily. She said that, of course, they had picked out the two gunmen, but had thought nothing of it when the man with the stick had gone to stand behind Bond's chair. They could not believe that anything would be attempted in the Casino itself. Directly Bond and Leiter had left to walk over to the hotel, she had telephoned Paris and told M's representative of the result of the game. She had had to speak guardedly and the agent had rung off without comment. She had been told to do this whatever the result. M had asked for the information to be passed on to him personally at any time of the day or night.

This was all she said. She sipped at her champagne and rarely glanced at Bond. She didn't smile. Bond felt frustrated. He drank a lot of champagne and ordered another bottle. The scrambled eggs came and they ate in silence.

At four o'clock Bond was about to call for the bill when the *maître d'hôtel* appeared at their table and inquired for Miss Lynd. He handed her a note which she took and read hastily.

'Oh, it's only Mathis,' she said. 'He says would I come to the entrance hall. He's got a message for you. Perhaps he's not in evening clothes or something. I won't be a minute. Then perhaps we could go home.'

She gave him a strained smile. 'I'm afraid I don't feel very good company this evening. It's been rather a nerve-racking day. I'm so sorry.'

Bond made a perfunctory reply and rose, pushing back the table. 'I'll get the bill,' he said, and watched her take the few steps to the entrance.

He sat down and lit a cigarette. He felt flat. He suddenly realized that he was tired. The stuffiness of the room hit him as it had hit him in the Casino in the early hours of the previous day. He called for the bill and took a last mouthful of champagne. It tasted bitter, as the first glass too many always does. He would have liked to have seen Mathis's cheerful face and heard his news, perhaps even a word of congratulation.

Suddenly the note to Vesper seemed odd to him. It was not the way Mathis would do things. He would have asked them both to join him at the bar of the Casino or he would have joined them in the night-club, whatever his clothes. They would have laughed together and Mathis would have been excited. He had much to tell Bond, more than Bond had to tell him. The arrest of the Bulgarian, who had probably talked some more; the chase after the man with the stick; Le Chiffre's movements when he left the Casino.

Bond shook himself. He hastily paid the bill, not waiting for the change. He pushed back his table and walked quickly through the entrance without acknowledging the good-nights of the *maître d'hôtel* and the doorman.

He hurried through the gaming-room and looked carefully up and down the long entrance hall. He cursed and quickened his step. There were only one or two officials and two or three men and women in evening clothes getting their things at the *vestiaire*.

No Vesper. No Mathis.

He was almost running. He got to the entrance and looked along the steps to left and right down and amongst the few remaining cars.

The commissionaire came towards him.

'A taxi, monsieur?'

Bond waved him aside and started down the steps, his eyes staring into the shadows, the night air cold on his sweating temples.

He was half-way down when he heard a faint cry, then the slam of a door way to the right. With a harsh growl and stutter from the exhaust a beetle-browed Citroën shot out of the shadows into the light of the moon, its front-wheel drive dry-skidding through the loose pebbles of the forecourt.

Its tail rocked on its soft springs as if a violent struggle was taking place on the back seat.

With a snarl it raced out to the wide entrance gate in a spray of gravel. A small black object shot out of an open rear window and thudded into a flower-bed. There was a scream of tortured rubber as the tyres caught the boulevard in a harsh left-handed turn, the deafening echo of a Citroën's exhaust in second gear, a crash into top, then a swiftly diminishing crackle as the car hared off between the shops on the main street towards the coast road.

Bond knew he would find Vesper's evening bag among the flowers.

He ran back with it across the gravel to the brightly-lit steps and scrabbled through its contents while the commissionaire hovered round him.

The crumpled note was there amongst the usual feminine baggage.

Can you come out to the entrance hall for a moment? I have news for your companion.

René Mathis

It was the crudest possible forgery.

Bond leapt for the Bentley, blessing the impulse which had made him drive it over after dinner. With the choke full out, the engine answered at once to the starter and the roar drowned the faltering words of the commissionaire who jumped aside as the rear wheels whipped gravel at his piped trouser-legs.

As the car rocked to the left outside the gate, Bond ruefully longed for the front-wheel drive and low chassis of the Citroën. Then he went fast through the gears and settled himself for the pursuit, briefly savouring the echo of the huge exhaust as it came back at him from either side of the short main street through the town.

Soon he was out on the coast road, a broad highway through the sand-dunes which he knew from his morning's drive had an excellent surface and was well cat's-eyed on the bends. He pushed the revs up and up, hurrying the car to eighty then to ninety, his huge Marchal headlights boring a safe white tunnel, nearly half a mile long, between the walls of the night.

He knew the Citroën must have come this way. He had heard the exhaust penetrate beyond the town, and a little dust still hung on the bends. He hoped soon to see the distant shaft of its headlights. The night was still and clear. Only out at sea there must be a light summer mist for at intervals he could hear the fog-horns lowing like iron cattle down the coast.

As he drove, whipping the car faster and faster through the night, with the other half of his mind he cursed Vesper, and M for having sent her on the job.

This was just what he had been afraid of. These blithering women who thought they could do a man's work. Why the hell couldn't they stay at home and mind their pots and pans and stick to their frocks and gossip and leave men's work to the men. And now for this to happen to him, just when the job had come off so beautifully. For Vesper to fall for an old trick like that and get herself snatched and probably held to ranson like some bloody heroine in a strip cartoon. The silly bitch.

Bond boiled at the thought of the fix he was in.

Of course. The idea was a straight swop. The girl against his cheque for forty million. Well, he wouldn't play: wouldn't think of playing. She was in the Service and knew what she was up against. He wouldn't even ask M. This job was more important than her. It was just too bad. She was a fine girl, but he wasn't going to fall for this childish trick. No dice. He would try and catch the Citroën and shoot it out with them and if she got shot in the process, that was too bad too. He would have done his stuff – tried to rescue her before they got her off to some hideout – but if he didn't catch up with them he would get back to his hotel and go to sleep and say no more about it. The next morning he would ask Mathis what had happened to her and show him the note. If Le Chiffre put the touch on Bond for the money in exchange for the girl, Bond would do nothing and tell no one. The girl would just have to take it. If the commissionaire came along with the story of what he had seen, Bond would bluff it out by saying he had had a drunken row with the girl.

Bond's mind raged furiously on with the problem as he flung the great car down the coast road, automatically taking the curves and watching out for carts or cyclists on their way into Royale. On straight stretches the Amherst Villiers supercharger dug spurs into the Bentley's twenty-five horses and the engine sent a high-pitched scream of pain into the night. Then the revolutions mounted until he was past 110 and on to the 120 mph mark on the speedometer.

He knew he must be gaining fast. Loaded as she was the Citroën could hardly better eighty even on this road. On an impulse he slowed down to seventy, turned on his foglights, and dowsed the twin Marchals. Sure enough, without the blinding curtain of his own lights, he could see the glow of another car a mile or two down the coast.

He felt under the dashboard and from a concealed holster took out a long-barrelled Colt Army Special .45

and laid it on the seat beside him. With this, if he was lucky with the surface of the road, he could hope to get their tyres or their petrol tank at anything up to a hundred yards.

Then he switched on the big lights again and screamed off in pursuit. He felt calm and at ease. The problem of Vesper's life was a problem no longer. His face in the blue light from the dashboard was grim but serene.

Ahead in the Citroën there were three men and the girl.

Le Chiffre was driving, his big fluid body hunched forward, his hands light and delicate on the wheel. Beside sat the squat man who had carried the stick in the Casino. In his left hand he grasped a thick lever which protruded beside him almost level with the floor. It might have been a lever to adjust the driving seat.

In the back seat was the tall thin gunman. He lay back relaxed, gazing at the ceiling, apparently uninterested in the wild speed of the car. His right hand lay caressingly on Vesper's left thigh which stretched out naked beside him.

Apart from her legs, which were naked to the hips, Vesper was only a parcel. Her long black velvet skirt had been lifted over her arms and head and tied above her head with a piece of rope. Where her face was, a small gap had been torn in the velvet so that she could breathe. She was not bound in any other way and she lay quiet, her body moving sluggishly with the swaying of the car.

Le Chiffre was concentrating half on the road ahead and half on the onrushing glare of Bond's headlights in the driving-mirror. He seemed undisturbed when not more than a mile separated the hare from the hounds and he even brought the car down from eighty to sixty miles an hour. Now, as he swept round a bend he slowed down still further. A few hundred yards ahead a Michelin post showed where a small parochial road crossed with the highway.

'*Attention*,' he said sharply to the man beside him.

The man's hand tightened on the lever.

A hundred yards from the cross-roads he slowed to thirty. In the mirror Bond's great headlights were lighting up the bend.

Le Chiffre seemed to make up his mind.

'*Allez*.'

The man beside him pulled the lever sharply upwards. The boot at the back of the car yawned open like a whale's mouth. There was a tinkling clatter on the road and then a rhythmic jangling as if the car was towing lengths of chain behind it.

'*Coupez*.'

The man depressed the lever sharply and the jangling stopped with a final clatter.

Le Chiffre glanced again in the mirror. Bond's car was just entering the bend. Le Chiffre made a racing change and threw the Citroën left-handed down the narrow side-road, at the same time dowsing his lights.

He stopped the car with a jerk and all three men got swiftly out and doubled back under cover of a low hedge to the cross-roads, now fiercely illuminated by the lights of the Bentley. Each of them carried a revolver and the thin man also had what looked like a large black egg in his right hand.

The Bentley screamed down towards them like an express train.

As Bond hurtled round the bend, caressing the great car against the camber with an easy sway of body and hands, he was working out his plan of action when the distance between the two cars had narrowed still further. He imagined that the enemy driver would try to dodge off into a side-road if he got the chance. So when he got round the bend and saw no lights ahead, it was a normal reflex to ease up on the accelerator and, when he saw the Michelin post, to prepare to brake.

He was only doing about sixty as he approached the black patch across the right-hand crown of the road which he assumed to be the shadow cast by a wayside tree. Even so, there was no time to save himself. There was suddenly a small carpet of glinting steel spikes right under his off-side wing. Then he was on top of it.

Bond automatically slammed the brakes full on and braced all his sinews against the wheel to correct the inevitable slew to the left, but he only kept control for a split second. As the rubber was flayed from his off-side wheels and the rims for an instant tore up the tarmac, the heavy car whirled across the road in a tearing dry skid, slammed the left bank with a crash that knocked Bond out of the driving-seat on to the floor, and then, facing back up the road, it reared slowly up, its front wheels spinning and its great headlights searching the sky. For a split second, resting on the petrol tank, it seemed to paw at the heavens like a giant praying-mantis. Then slowly it toppled over backwards and fell with a splintering crash of coachwork and glass.

In the deafening silence, the near-side front wheel whispered briefly on and then squeaked to a stop.

Le Chiffre and his two men only had to walk a few yards from their ambush.

'Put your guns away and get him out,' he ordered brusquely. 'I'll keep you covered. Be careful of him. I don't want a corpse. And hurry up, it's getting light.'

The two men got down on their knees. One of them took out a long knife and cut some of the fabric away from the side of the convertible hood and took hold of Bond's shoulders. He was unconscious and immovable. The other squeezed between the upturned car and the bank and forced his way through the crumpled window-frame. He eased Bond's legs, pinned between the steering-wheel and the fabric roof of the car. Then they inched him out through a hole in the hood.

They were sweating and filthy with dust and oil by the time they had him lying in the road.

The thin man felt his heart and then slapped his face hard on either side. Bond grunted and moved a hand. The thin man slapped him again.

'That's enough,' said Le Chiffre. 'Tie his arms and

put him in the car. Here,' he threw a roll of flex to the man. 'Empty his pockets first and give me his gun. He may have got some other weapons, but we can get them later.'

He took the objects the thin man handed him and stuffed them and Bond's Beretta into his wide pockets without examining them. He left the men to it and walked back to the car. His face showed neither pleasure nor excitement.

It was the sharp bite of the wire flex into his wrists that brought Bond to himself. He was aching all over as if he had been thrashed with a wooden club, but when he was yanked to his feet and pushed towards the narrow side-road where the engine of the Citroën was already running softly, he found that no bones were broken. But he felt in no mood for desperate attempts to escape and allowed himself to be dragged into the back seat of the car without resisting.

He felt thoroughly dispirited and weak in resolve as well as in his body. He had had to take too much in the past twenty-four hours and now this last stroke by the enemy seemed almost too final. This time there could be no miracles. No one knew where he was and no one would miss him until well on into the morning. The wreck of his car would be found before very long, but it would take hours to trace the ownership to him.

And Vesper. He looked to the right, past the thin man who was lying back with his eyes closed. His first reaction was one of scorn. Damn fool girl getting herself trussed up like a chicken, having her skirt pulled over her head as if the whole of this business was some kind of dormitory rag. But then he felt sorry for her. Her naked legs looked so childlike and defenceless.

'Vesper,' he said softly.

There was no answer from the bundle in the corner and Bond suddenly had a chill feeling, but then she stirred slightly.

At the same time the thin man caught him a hard backhanded blow over the heart.

'Silence.'

Bond doubled over with the pain and to shield himself from another blow, only to get a rabbit punch on the back of the neck which made him arch back again, the breath whistling through his teeth.

The thin man had hit him a hard professional cutting blow with the edge of the hand. There was something rather deadly about his accuracy and lack of effort. He was now again lying back, his eyes closed. He was a man to make you afraid, an evil man. Bond hoped he might get a chance of killing him.

Suddenly the boot of the car was thrown open and there was a clanking crash. Bond guessed that they had been waiting for the third man to retrieve the carpet of spiked chain-mail. He assumed it must be an adaptation of the nail-studded devices used by the Resistance against German staff-cars.

Again he reflected on the efficiency of these people and the ingenuity of the equipment they used. Had

M underestimated their resourcefulness? He stifled a desire to place the blame on London. It was he who should have known; he who should have been warned by small signs and taken infinitely more precautions. He squirmed as he thought of himself washing down champagne in the Roi Galant while the enemy was busy preparing his counter-stroke. He cursed himself and cursed the *hubris* which had made him so sure the battle was won and the enemy in flight.

All this time Le Chiffre had said nothing. Directly the boot was shut, the third man, whom Bond at once recognized, climbed in beside him and Le Chiffre reversed furiously back on to the main road. Then he banged the gear lever through the gate and was soon doing seventy on down the coast.

By now it was dawn – about five o'clock, Bond guessed – and he reflected that a mile or two on was the turning to Le Chiffre's villa. He had not thought that they would take Vesper there. Now that he realized that Vesper had only been a sprat to catch a mackerel the whole picture became clear.

It was an extremely unpleasant picture. For the first time since his capture, fear came to Bond and crawled up his spine.

Ten minutes later the Citroën lurched to the left, ran on a hundred yards up a small side-road partly overgrown with grass and then between a pair of dilapidated stucco pillars into an unkempt forecourt surrounded by a high wall. They drew up in front of a peeling white door. Above a rusty bell-push in the door-frame, small zinc letters on a wooden base spelled out 'Les Noctambules' and, underneath, 'Sonnez SVP'.

From what Bond could see of the cement frontage, the villa was typical of the French seaside style. He could imagine the dead blue-bottles being hastily swept out for the summer let and the stale rooms briefly aired by a cleaning woman sent by the estate agent in Royale. Every five years one coat of whitewash would be slapped over the rooms and the outside woodwork, and for a few weeks the villa would present a smiling front to the world. Then the winter rains would get to work, and the imprisoned flies, and quickly the villa would take on again its abandoned look.

But, Bond reflected, it would admirably serve Le Chiffre's purpose this morning, if he was right in assuming what that was to be. They had passed no other house since his capture and from his reconnaissance of the day before he knew there was only an occasional farm for several miles to the south.

As he was urged out of the car with a sharp crack in the ribs from the thin man's elbow, he knew that Le Chiffre could have them both to himself, undisturbed, for several hours. Again his skin crawled.

Le Chiffre opened the door with a key and disappeared inside. Vesper, looking incredibly indecent in the early light of day, was pushed in after him with a torrent of lewd French from the man whom Bond knew to himself as 'the Corsican'. Bond followed without giving the thin man a chance to urge him.

The key of the front door turned in the lock.

Le Chiffre was standing in the doorway of a room on the right. He crooked a finger at Bond in a silent, spidery summons.

Vesper was being led down a passage towards the back of the house. Bond suddenly decided.

With a wild backward kick which connected with the thin man's shins and brought a whistle of pain from him he hurled himself down the passage after her. With only his feet as weapons, there was no plan in his mind except to do as much damage as possible to the two gunmen and be able to exchange a few hurried words with the girl. No other plan was possible. He just wanted to tell her not to give in.

As the Corsican turned at the commotion Bond was on him and his right shoe was launched in a flying kick at the other man's groin.

Like lightning the Corsican slammed himself back against the wall of the passage and, as Bond's foot whistled past his hip, he very quickly, but somehow delicately, shot out his left hand, caught Bond's shoe at the top of its arch and twisted it sharply.

Completely off balance, Bond's other foot left the ground. In the air his whole body turned and with the momentum of his rush behind it crashed sideways and down on to the floor.

For a moment he lay there, all the breath knocked

out of him. Then the thin man came and hauled him up against the wall by his collar. He had a gun in his hand. He looked Bond inquisitively in the eyes. Then unhurriedly he bent down and swiped the barrel viciously across Bond's shins. Bond grunted and caved at the knees.

'If there is a next time, it will be across your teeth,' said the thin man in bad French.

A door slammed. Vesper and the Corsican had disappeared. Bond turned his head to the right. Le Chiffre had moved a few feet out into the passage. He lifted his finger and crooked it again. Then for the first time he spoke.

'Come, my dear friend. We are wasting our time.'

He spoke in English with no accent. His voice was low and soft and unhurried. He showed no emotion. He might have been a doctor summoning the next patient from the waiting-room, a hysterical patient who had been expostulating feebly with a nurse.

Bond again felt puny and impotent. Nobody but an expert in ju-jitsu could have handled him with the Corsican's economy and lack of fuss. The cold precision with which the thin man had paid him back in his own coin had been equally unhurried, even artistic.

Almost docilely Bond walked back down the passage. He had nothing but a few more bruises to show for his clumsy gesture of resistance to these people.

As he preceded the thin man over the threshold he knew that he was utterly and absolutely in their power.

17 / 'MY DEAR BOY'

It was a large bare room, sparsely furnished in cheap French *art nouveau* style. It was difficult to say whether it was intended as a living- or dining-room for a flimsy-looking mirrored sideboard, sporting an orange crackleware fruit dish and two painted wooden candlesticks, took up most of the wall opposite the door and contradicted the faded pink sofa ranged against the other side of the room.

There was no table in the centre under the alabasterine ceiling light, only a small square of stained carpet with a futurist design in contrasting browns.

Over by the window was an incongruous-looking throne-like chair in carved oak with a red velvet seat, a low table on which stood an empty water carafe and two glasses, and a light arm-chair with a round cane seat and no cushion.

Half-closed venetian blinds obscured the view from the window, but cast bars of early sunlight over the few pieces of furniture and over part of the brightly papered wall and the brown stained floorboards.

Le Chiffre pointed at the cane chair.

'That will do excellently,' he said to the thin man.

'Prepare him quickly. If he resists, damage him only a little.'

He turned to Bond. There was no expression on his large face and his round eyes were uninterested. 'Take off your clothes. For every effort to resist, Basil will break one of your fingers. We are serious people and your good health is of no interest to us. Whether you live or die depends on the outcome of the talk we are about to have.'

He made a gesture towards the thin man and left the room.

The thin man's first action was a curious one. He opened the clasp-knife he had used on the hood of Bond's car, took the small arm-chair and with a swift motion he cut out its cane seat.

Then he came back to Bond, sticking the still open knife, like a fountain-pen, in the vest pocket of his coat. He turned Bond round to the light and unwound the flex from his wrists. Then he stood quickly aside and the knife was back in his right hand.

'*Vite.*'

Bond stood chafing his swollen wrists and debating with himself how much time he could waste by resisting. He only delayed an instant. With a swift step and a downward sweep of his free hand, the thin man seized the collar of his dinner-jacket and dragged it down, pinning Bond's arms back. Bond made the traditional counter to this old policeman's hold by dropping down on one knee, but as he dropped the thin man dropped with him and at the same time brought his knife round and down behind Bond's back. Bond felt the back of the blade pass down his spine. There was the hiss of a sharp knife through cloth and his arms were suddenly free as the two halves of his coat fell forward.

He cursed and stood up. The thin man was back in his previous position, his knife again at the ready in his relaxed hand. Bond let the two halves of his dinner-jacket fall off his arms on to the floor.

'*Allez,*' said the thin man with a faint trace of impatience.

Bond looked him in the eye and then slowly started to take off his shirt.

Le Chiffre came quietly back into the room. He carried a pot of what smelt like coffee. He put it on the small table near the window. He also placed beside it on the table two other homely objects, a three-foot-long carpet-beater in twisted cane and a carving knife.

He settled himself comfortably on the throne-like chair and poured some of the coffee into one of the glasses. With one foot he hooked forward the small arm-chair, whose seat was now an empty circular frame of wood, until it was directly opposite him.

Bond stood stark naked in the middle of the room, bruises showing livid on his white body, his face a grey mask of exhaustion and knowledge of what was to come.

'Sit down there.' Le Chiffre nodded at the chair in front of him.

Bond walked over and sat down.

The thin man produced some flex. With this he bound Bond's wrists to the arms of the chair and his ankles to the front legs. He passed a double strand across his chest, under the arm-pits and through the chair-back. He made no mistakes with the knots and left no play in any of the bindings. All of them bit sharply into Bond's flesh. The legs of the chair were broadly spaced and Bond could not even rock it.

He was utterly a prisoner, naked and defenceless.

His buttocks and the underpart of his body protruded through the seat of the chair towards the floor.

Le Chiffre nodded to the thin man who quietly left the room and closed the door.

There was a packet of Gauloises on the table and a lighter. Le Chiffre lit a cigarette and swallowed a mouthful of coffee from the glass. Then he picked up the cane carpet-beater and, resting the handle comfortably on his knee, allowed the flat trefoil base to lie on the floor directly under Bond's chair.

He looked Bond carefully, almost caressingly, in the eyes. Then his wrists sprang suddenly upwards on his knee.

The result was startling.

Bond's whole body arched in an involuntary spasm. His face contracted in a soundless scream and his lips drew right away from his teeth. At the same time his head flew back with a jerk showing the taut sinews of his neck. For an instant, muscles stood out in knots all over his body and his toes and fingers clenched until they were quite white. Then his body sagged and perspiration started to bead all over his body. He uttered a deep groan.

Le Chiffre waited for his eyes to open.

'You see, dear boy?' He smiled a soft, fat smile. 'Is the position quite clear now?'

A drop of sweat fell off Bond's chin on to his naked chest.

'Now let us get down to business and see how soon we can be finished with this unfortunate mess you have got yourself into.' He puffed cheerfully at his cigarette and gave an admonitory tap on the floor beneath Bond's chair with his horrible and incongruous instrument.

'My dear boy,' Le Chiffre spoke like a father, 'the game of Red Indians is over, quite over. You have stumbled by mischance into a game for grown-ups and you have already found it a painful experience. You are not equipped, my dear boy, to play games with adults and it was very foolish of your nanny in London to have sent you out here with your spade and bucket. Very foolish indeed and most unfortunate for you.

'But we must stop joking, my dear fellow, although I am sure you would like to follow me in developing this amusing little cautionary tale.'

He suddenly dropped his bantering tone and looked at Bond sharply and venomously.

'Where is the money?'

Bond's bloodshot eyes looked emptily back at him.

Again the upward jerk of the wrist and again Bond's whole body writhed and contorted.

Le Chiffre waited until the tortured heart eased down its laboured pumping and until Bond's eyes dully opened again.

'Perhaps I should explain,' said Le Chiffre. 'I intend to continue attacking the sensitive parts of your body until you answer my question. I am without mercy and there will be no relenting. There is no one to stage a last-minute rescue and there is no possibility of escape for you. This is not a romantic adventure story in which the villain is finally routed and the hero is given a medal and marries the girl. Unfortunately these things don't happen in real life. If you continue to be obstinate, you will be tortured to the edge of madness and then the girl will be brought in and we will set about her in front of you. If that is still not enough, you will both be painfully killed and I shall reluctantly leave your bodies and make my way abroad to a comfortable house which is waiting for me. There I shall take up a useful and profitable career and live to a ripe and peaceful old age in the bosom of the family I shall doubtless create. So you see, my dear boy, that I stand to lose nothing. If you hand the money over, so much the better. If not, I shall shrug my shoulders and be on my way.'

He paused, and his wrist lifted slightly on his knee. Bond's flesh cringed as the cane surface just touched him.

'But you, my dear fellow, can only hope that I shall spare you further pain and spare your life. There is no other hope for you but that. Absolutely none.

'Well?'

Bond closed his eyes and waited for the pain. He knew that the beginning of torture is the worst. There is a parabola of agony. A crescendo leading up to a peak and then the nerves are blunted and react progressively less until unconsciousness and death. All he could do was to pray for the peak, pray that his spirit would hold out so long and then accept the long free-wheel down to the final black-out.

He had been told by colleagues who had survived torture by the Germans and the Japanese that towards the end there came a wonderful period of warmth and languor leading into a sort of sexual twilight where pain turned to pleasure and where hatred and fear of the torturers turned to a masochistic infatuation. It was the supreme test of will, he had learnt, to avoid showing this form of punch-drunkenness. Directly it was suspected they would either kill you at once and save themselves further useless effort, or let you recover sufficiently so that your nerves had crept back to the other side of the parabola. Then they would start again.

He opened his eyes a fraction.

Le Chiffre had been waiting for this and like a rattle-snake the cane instrument leapt from the floor. It struck again and again so that Bond screamed and his body jangled in the chair like a marionette.

Le Chiffre desisted only when Bond's tortured spasms showed a trace of sluggishness. He sat for a while sipping his coffee and frowning slightly like a surgeon watching a cardiograph during a difficult operation.

When Bond's eyes flickered and opened he addressed him again, but now with a trace of impatience.

'We know that the money is somewhere in your room,' he said. 'You drew a cheque to cash for forty million francs and I know that you went back to the hotel to hide it.'

For a moment Bond wondered how he had been so certain.

'Directly you left for the night club,' continued Le Chiffre, 'your room was searched by four of my people.'

The Muntzes must have helped, reflected Bond.

'We found a good deal in childish hiding-places. The ball-cock in the lavatory yielded an interesting little codebook and we found some more of your papers taped to the back of a drawer. All the furniture has been taken to pieces and your clothes and the curtains and bedclothes have been cut up. Every inch of the room has been searched and all the fittings removed. It is most unfortunate for you that we didn't find the cheque. If we had, you would now be comfortably in bed, perhaps with the beautiful Miss Lynd, instead of this.' He lashed upwards.

Through the red mist of pain, Bond thought of Vesper. He could imagine how she was being used by the two gunmen. They would be making the most of her before she was sent for by Le Chiffre. He thought of the fat wet lips of the Corsican and the slow cruelty of the thin man. Poor wretch to have been dragged into this. Poor little beast.

Le Chiffre was talking again.

'Torture is a terrible thing,' he was saying as he puffed at a fresh cigarette, 'but it is a simple matter for the torturer, particularly when the patient,' he smiled at the word, 'is a man. You see, my dear Bond, with a man it is quite unnecessary to indulge in refinements. With this simple instrument, or with almost any other object, one can cause a man as much pain as is possible or necessary. Do not believe what you read in novels or books about the war. There is nothing worse. It is not only the immediate agony, but also the thought that your manhood is being gradually destroyed and that at the end, if you will not yield, you will no longer be a man.

'That, my dear Bond, is a sad and terrible thought – a long chain of agony for the body and also for the mind, and then the final screaming moment when you will beg me to kill you. All that is inevitable unless you tell me where you hid the money.'

He poured some more coffee into the glass and drank it down leaving brown corners to his mouth.

Bond's lips were writhing. He was trying to say something. At last he got the word out in a harsh croak: 'Drink,' he said and his tongue came out and swilled across his dry lips.

'Of course, my dear boy, how thoughtless of me.' Le Chiffre poured some coffee into the other glass. There was a ring of sweat drops on the floor round Bond's chair.

'We must certainly keep your tongue lubricated.'

He laid the handle of the carpet-beater down on the floor between his thick legs and rose from his chair. He went behind Bond and taking a handful of his soaking hair in one hand, he wrenched Bond's head sharply back. He poured the coffee down Bond's throat in small mouthfuls so that he would not choke. Then he released his head so that it fell forward again on his chest. He went back to his chair and picked up the carpet-beater.

Bond raised his head and spoke thickly.

'Money no good to you.' His voice was a laborious croak. 'Police trace it to you.'

Exhausted by the effort, his head sank forward again. He was a little, but only a little, exaggerating the extent of his physical collapse. Anything to gain time and anything to defer the next searing pain.

'Ah, my dear fellow, I had forgotten to tell you.' Le

Chiffre smiled wolfishly. 'We met after our little game at the Casino and you were such a sportsman that you agreed we would have one more run through the pack between the two of us. It was a gallant gesture. Typical of an English gentleman.

'Unfortunately you lost and this upset you so much that you decided to leave Royale immediately for an unknown destination. Like the gentleman you are, you very kindly gave me a note explaining the circumstances so that I would have no difficulty in cashing your cheque. You see, dear boy, everything has been thought of and you need have no fears on my account.' He chuckled fatly.

'Now shall we continue? I have all the time in the world and truth to tell I am rather interested to see how long a man can stand this particular form of . . . er . . . encouragement.' He rattled the harsh cane on the floor.

So that was the score, thought Bond, with a final sinking of the heart. The 'unknown destination' would be under the ground or under the sea, or perhaps, more simply, under the crashed Bentley. Well, if he had to die anyway, he might as well try it the hard way. He had no hope that Mathis or Leiter would get to him in time, but at least there was a chance that they would catch up with Le Chiffre before he could get away. It must be getting on for seven. The car might have been found by now. It was a choice of evils, but the longer Le Chiffre continued the torture the more likely he would be revenged.

Bond lifted his head and looked Le Chiffre in the eyes.

The china of the whites was now veined with red. It was like looking at two blackcurrants poached in blood. The rest of the wide face was yellowish except where a thick black stubble covered the moist skin. The upward edges of black coffee at the corners of the mouth gave his expression a false smile and the whole face was faintly striped by the light through the venetian blinds.

'No,' he said flatly, ' . . . you . . .'

Le Chiffre grunted and set to work again with savage fury. Occasionally he snarled like a wild beast.

After ten minutes Bond had fainted, blessedly.

Le Chiffre at once stopped. He wiped some sweat from his face with a circular motion of his disengaged hand. Then he looked at his watch and seemed to make up his mind.

He got up and stood behind the inert, dripping body. There was no colour in Bond's face or anywhere on his body above the waist. There was a faint flutter of his skin above the heart. Otherwise he might have been dead.

Le Chiffre seized Bond's ears and harshly twisted them. Then he leant forward and slapped his cheeks hard several times. Bond's head rolled from side to side with each blow. Slowly his breathing became deeper. An animal groan came from his lolling mouth.

Le Chiffre took a glass of coffee and poured some

into Bond's mouth and threw the rest in his face. Bond's eyes slowly opened.

Le Chiffre returned to his chair and waited. He lit a cigarette and contemplated the spattered pool of blood on the floor beneath the inert body opposite.

Bond groaned again pitifully. It was an inhuman sound. His eyes opened and he gazed dully at his torturer.

Le Chiffre spoke.

'That is all, Bond. We will now finish with you. You understand? Not kill you, but finish with you. And then we will have in the girl and see if something can be got out of the remains of the two of you.'

He reached towards the table.

'Say good-bye to it, Bond.'

It was extraordinary to hear the third voice. The hour's ritual had only demanded a duologue against the horrible noise of the torture. Bond's dimmed senses hardly took it in. Then suddenly he was half-way back to consciousness. He found he could see and hear again. He could hear the dead silence after the one quiet word from the doorway. He could see Le Chiffre's head slowly come up and the expression of blank astonishment, of innocent amazement, slowly give way to fear.

'Shtop,' had said the voice, quietly.

Bond heard slow steps approaching behind his chair.

'Dhrop it,' said the voice.

Bond saw Le Chiffre's hand open obediently and the knife fall with a clatter to the floor.

He tried desperately to read into Le Chiffre's face what was happening behind him, but all he saw was blind incomprehension and terror. Le Chiffre's mouth worked, but only a high-pitched 'eek' came from it. His heavy cheeks trembled as he tried to collect enough saliva in his mouth to say something, ask something. His hands fluttered vaguely in his lap. One of them made a slight movement towards his pocket, but instantly fell back. His round staring eyes had lowered for a split second and Bond guessed there was a gun trained on him.

There was a moment's silence.

'SMERSH.'

The word came almost with a sigh. It came with a downward cadence as if nothing else had to be said. It was the final explanation. The last word of all.

'No,' said Le Chiffre. 'No. I . . .' His voice tailed off.

Perhaps he was going to explain, to apologize, but what he must have seen in the other's face made it all useless.

'Your two men. Both dead. You are a fool and a thief and a traitor. I have been sent from the Soviet Union to eliminate you. You are fortunate that I have only time to shoot you. If it was possible, I was instructed that you should die most painfully. We cannot see the end of the trouble you have caused.'

The thick voice stopped. There was silence in the room save for the rasping breath of Le Chiffre.

Somewhere outside a bird began to sing and there were other small noises from the awakening country-side. The bands of sunlight were stronger and the sweat on Le Chiffre's face glistened brightly.

'Do you plead guilty?'

Bond wrestled with his consciousness. He screwed up his eyes and tried to shake his head to clear it, but his whole nervous system was numbed and no message was transmitted to his muscles. He could just keep his focus on the great pale face in front of him and on its bulging eyes.

A thin string of saliva crept from the open mouth and hung down from the chin.

'Yes,' said the mouth.

There was a sharp 'phut', no louder than a bubble of air escaping from a tube of toothpaste. No other noise at all, and suddenly Le Chiffre had grown another eye, a third eye on a level with the other two, right where the thick nose started to jut out below the forehead. It was a small black eye, without eyelashes or eyebrows.

For a second the three eyes looked out across the room and then the whole face seemed to slip and go down on one knee. The two outer eyes turned trembling up towards the ceiling. Then the heavy head fell sideways and the right shoulder and finally the whole upper part of the body lurched over the arm of the chair as if Le Chiffre were going to be sick. But there was only a short rattle of his heels on the ground and then no other movement.

The tall back of the chair looked impassively out across the dead body in its arms.

There was a faint movement behind Bond. A hand came from behind and grasped his chin and pulled it back.

For a moment Bond looked up into two glittering eyes behind a narrow black mask. There was the impression of a crag-like face under a hat-brim, the collar of a fawn mackintosh. He could take in nothing more before his head was pushed down again.

'You are fortunate,' said the voice. 'I have no orders to kill you. Your life has been saved twice in one day. But you can tell your organization that SMERSH is only merciful by chance or by mistake. In your case you were saved first by chance and now by mistake, for I should have had orders to kill any foreign spies who were hanging round this traitor like flies round a dog's mess.

'But I shall leave you my visiting-card. You are a gambler. You play at cards. One day perhaps you will play against one of us. It would be well that you should be known as a spy.'

Steps moved round to behind Bond's right shoulder. There was the click of a knife opening. An arm in some grey material came into Bond's line of vision. A broad hairy hand emerging from a dirty white shirt-cuff was holding a thin stiletto like a fountain-pen. It poised for a moment above the back of Bond's right hand, immovably bound with flex to the arm of the chair. The point of the stiletto executed three quick straight slashes. A fourth slash crossed them where they ended, just short of the knuckles. Blood in the shape of an inverted 'M' welled out and slowly started to drip on to the floor.

The pain was nothing to what Bond was already suffering, but it was enough to plunge him again into unconsciousness.

The steps moved quietly away across the room. The door was softly closed.

In the silence, the cheerful small sounds of the summer's day crept through the closed window. High on the left-hand wall hung two small patches of pink light. They were reflections cast upwards from the floor by the zebra stripes of June sunshine, cast upwards from two separate pools of blood a few feet apart.

As the day progressed the pink patches marched slowly along the wall. And slowly they grew larger.

You are about to awake when you dream that you are dreaming.

During the next two days James Bond was permanently in this state without regaining consciousness. He watched the procession of his dreams go by without any effort to disturb their sequence, although many of them were terrifying and all were painful. He knew that he was in a bed and that he was lying on his back and could not move and in one of his twilight moments he thought there were people round him, but he made no effort to open his eyes and re-enter the world.

He felt safer in the darkness and he hugged it to him.

On the morning of the third day a bloody nightmare shook him awake, trembling and sweating. There was a hand on his forehead which he associated with his dream. He tried to lift an arm and smash it sideways into the owner of the hand, but his arms were immovable, secured to the sides of his bed. His whole body was strapped down and something like a large white coffin covered him from chest to feet and obscured his view of the end of the bed. He shouted a string of obscenities, but the effort took all his strength and the words tailed off into a sob. Tears of forlornness and self-pity welled out of his eyes.

A woman's voice was speaking and the words gradually penetrated to him. It seemed to be a kind voice and it slowly came to him that he was being comforted and that this was a friend and not an enemy. He could hardly believe it. He had been so certain that he was still a captive and that the torture was about to begin again. He felt his face being softly wiped with a cool cloth which smelt of lavender and then he sank back into his dreams.

When he awoke again some hours later all his terrors had gone and he felt warm and languorous. Sun was streaming into the bright room and garden sounds came through the window. In the background there was the noise of small waves on a beach. As he moved his head he heard a rustle, and a nurse who had been sitting beside his pillow rose and came into his line of vision. She was pretty and she smiled as she put her hand on his pulse.

'Well, I'm certainly glad you've woken up at last. I've never heard such dreadful language in my life.'

Bond smiled back at her.

'Where am I?' he asked and was surprised that his voice sounded firm and clear.

'You're in a nursing home at Royale and I've been sent over from England to look after you. There are two of us and I'm Nurse Gibson. Now just lie quiet and I'll go and tell the doctor you're awake. You've been unconscious since they brought you in and we've been quite worried.'

Bond closed his eyes and mentally explored his body. The worst pain was in his wrists and ankles and in his right hand where the Russian had cut him. In the centre of the body there was no feeling. He assumed that he had been given a local anaesthetic. The rest of his body ached dully as if he had been beaten all over. He could feel the pressure of bandages everywhere and his unshaven neck and chin prickled against the sheets. From the feel of the bristles he knew that he must have been at least three days without shaving. That meant two days since the morning of the torture.

He was preparing a short list of questions in his mind when the door opened and the doctor came in followed by the nurse and in the background the dear figure of Mathis, a Mathis looking anxious behind his broad smile, who put a finger to his lips and walked on tiptoe to the window and sat down.

The doctor, a Frenchman with a young and intelligent face, had been detached from his duties with the Deuxième Bureau to look after Bond's case. He came and stood beside Bond and put his hand on Bond's forehead while he looked at the temperature chart behind the bed.

When he spoke he was forthright.

'You have a lot of questions to ask, my dear Mr Bond,' he said in excellent English, 'and I can tell you most of the answers. I do not want you to waste your strength, so I will give you the salient facts and then you may have a few minutes with Monsieur Mathis who wishes to obtain one or two details from you. It is really too early for this talk, but I wish to set your mind at rest so that we can proceed with the task of repairing your body without bothering too much about your mind.'

Nurse Gibson pulled up a chair for the doctor and left the room.

'You have been here about two days,' continued the doctor. 'Your car was found by a farmer on the way to market in Royale and he informed the police. After some delay Monsieur Mathis heard that it was your car and he immediately went to Les Noctambules with his men. You and Le Chiffre were found and also your friend, Miss Lynd, who was unharmed and according to her account suffered no molestation. She was prostrated with shock, but is now fully recovered and is at her hotel. She has been instructed by her superiors in London to stay at Royale under your orders until you are sufficiently recovered to go back to England.

'Le Chiffre's two gunmen are dead, each killed by a single .35 bullet in the back of the skull. From the lack of expression on their faces, they evidently never saw or heard their assailant. They were found in the same room as Miss Lynd. Le Chiffre is dead, shot with a similar weapon between the eyes. Did you witness his death?'

'Yes,' said Bond.

'Your own injuries are serious, but your life is not in

danger though you have lost a lot of blood. If all goes well, you will recover completely and none of the functions of your body will be impaired.' The doctor smiled grimly. 'But I fear that you will continue to be in pain for several days and it will be my endeavour to give you as much comfort as possible. Now that you have regained consciousness your arms will be freed, but you must not move your body and when you sleep the nurse has orders to secure your arms again. Above all, it is important that you rest and regain your strength. At the moment you are suffering from a grave condition of mental and physical shock.' The doctor paused. 'For how long were you maltreated?'

'About an hour,' said Bond.

'Then it is remarkable that you are alive and I congratulate you. Few men could have supported what you have been through. Perhaps that is some consolation. As Monsieur Mathis can tell you, I have had in my time to treat a number of patients who have suffered similar handling and not one has come through it as you have done.'

The doctor looked at Bond for a moment and then turned brusquely to Mathis.

'You may have ten minutes and then you will be forcibly ejected. If you put the patient's temperature up, you will answer for it.'

He gave them both a broad smile and left the room.

Mathis came over and took the doctor's chair.

'That's a good man,' said Bond. 'I like him.'

'He's attached to the Bureau,' said Mathis. 'He is a very good man and I will tell you about him one of these days. He thinks you are a prodigy – and so do I.

'However, that can wait. As you can imagine, there is much to clear up and I am being pestered by Paris and, of course, London, and even by Washington via our good friend Leiter. Incidentally,' he broke off, 'I have a personal message from M. He spoke to me himself on the telephone. He simply said to tell you that he is much impressed. I asked if that was all and he said: "Well, tell him that the Treasury is greatly relieved." Then he rang off.'

Bond grinned with pleasure. What most warmed him was that M himself should have rung up Mathis. This was quite unheard of. The very existence of M, let alone his identity, was never admitted. He could imagine the flutter this must have caused in the ultra-security-minded organization in London.

'A tall thin man with one arm came over from London the same day we found you,' continued Mathis, knowing from his own experience that these shop details would interest Bond more than anything else and give him most pleasure, 'and he fixed up the nurses and looked after everything. Even your car's being repaired for you. He seemed to be Vesper's boss. He spent a lot of time with her and gave her strict instructions to look after you.'

Head of S, thought Bond. They're certainly giving me the red carpet treatment.

'Now,' said Mathis, 'to business. Who killed Le Chiffre?'

'SMERSH,' said Bond.

Mathis gave a low whistle.

'My God,' he said respectfully. 'So they *were* on to him. What did he look like?'

Bond explained briefly what had happened up to the moment of Le Chiffre's death, omitting all but the most essential details. It cost him an effort and he was glad when it was done. Casting his mind back to the scene awoke the whole nightmare and the sweat began to pour off his forehead and a deep throb of pain started up in his body.

Mathis realized that he was going too far. Bond's voice was getting feebler and his eyes were clouding. Mathis snapped shut his shorthand book and laid a hand on Bond's shoulder.

'Forgive me, my friend,' he said. 'It is all over now and you are in safe hands. All is well and the whole plan has gone splendidly. We have announced that Le Chiffre shot his two accomplices and then committed suicide because he could not face an inquiry into the union funds. Strasbourg and the north are in an uproar. He was considered a great hero there and a pillar of the Communist Party in France. This story of brothels and casinos has absolutely knocked the bottom out of his organization and they're all running around like scalded cats. At the moment the Communist Party is giving out that he was off his head. But that hasn't helped much after Thorez's breakdown not long ago. They're just making it look as if all their big shots were gaga. God knows how they're going to unscramble the whole business.'

Mathis saw that his enthusiasm had had the desired effect. Bond's eyes were brighter.

'One last mystery,' Mathis said, 'and then I promise I will go.' He looked at his watch. 'The doctor will be after my skin in a moment. Now, what about the money? Where is it? Where did you hide it? We too have been over your room with a toothcomb. It isn't there.'

Bond grinned.

'It is,' he said, 'more or less. On the door of each room there is a small square of black plastic with the number of the room on it. On the corridor side, of course. When Leiter left me that night, I simply opened the door and unscrewed my number plate and put the folded cheque underneath it and screwed the plate back. It'll still be there.' He smiled. 'I'm glad there's something the stupid English can teach the clever French.'

Mathis laughed delightedly.

'I suppose you think that's paid me back for knowing what the Muntzes were up to. Well, I'll call it quits. Incidentally, we've got them in the bag. They were just some minor fry hired for the occasion. We'll see they get a few years.'

He rose hastily as the doctor stormed into the room and took one look at Bond.

'Out,' he said to Mathis. 'Out and don't come back.'

Mathis just had time to wave cheerfully to Bond and call some hasty words of farewell before he was hustled through the door. Bond heard a torrent of heated French diminishing down the corridor. He lay back exhausted, but heartened by all he had heard. He found himself thinking of Vesper as he quickly drifted off into a troubled sleep.

There were still questions to be answered, but they could wait.

Bond made good progress. When Mathis came to see him three days later he was propped up in bed and his arms were free. The lower half of his body was still shrouded in the oblong tent, but he looked cheerful and it was only occasionally that a twinge of pain narrowed his eyes.

Mathis looked crestfallen.

'Here's your cheque,' he said to Bond. 'I've rather enjoyed walking around with forty million francs in my pocket, but I suppose you'd better sign it and I'll put it to your account with the Crédit Lyonnais. There's no sign of our friend from SMERSH. Not a damn trace. He must have got to the villa on foot or on a bicycle because you heard nothing of his arrival and the two gunmen obviously didn't. It's pretty exasperating. We've got precious little on this SMERSH organization and neither has London. Washington said they had, but it turned out to be the usual waffle from refugee interrogation, and you know that's about as much good as interrogating an English man-in-the street about his own Secret Service, or a Frenchman about the Deuxième.'

'He probably came from Leningrad to Berlin via

Warsaw,' said Bond. 'From Berlin they've got plenty of routes open to the rest of Europe. He's back home by now being told off for not shooting me too. I fancy they've got quite a file on me in view of one or two of the jobs M's given me since the war. He obviously thought he was being smart enough cutting his initial in my hand.'

'What's that?' asked Mathis. 'The doctor said the cuts looked like a square M with a tail to the top. He said they didn't mean anything.'

'Well, I only got a glimpse before I passed out, but I've seen the cuts several times while they were being dressed and I'm pretty certain they are the Russian letter for SH. It's rather like an inverted M with a tail. That would make sense; SMERSH is short for SMYERT SHPIONAM – Death to Spies – and he thinks he's labelled me as a SHPION. It's a nuisance because M will probably say I've got to go to hospital again when I get back to London and have new skin grafted over the whole of the back of my hand. It doesn't matter much. I've decided to resign.'

Mathis looked at him with his mouth open.

'Resign?' he asked incredulously. 'What the hell for?'

Bond looked away from Mathis. He studied his bandaged hands.

'When I was being beaten up,' he said, 'I suddenly liked the idea of being alive. Before Le Chiffre began, he used a phrase which stuck in my mind . . . "playing

Red Indians". He said that's what I had been doing. Well, I suddenly thought he might be right.

'You see,' he said, still looking down at his bandages, 'when one's young, it seems very easy to distinguish between right and wrong, but as one gets older it becomes more difficult. At school it's easy to pick out one's own villains and heroes and one grows up wanting to be a hero and kill the villains.'

He looked obstinately at Mathis.

'Well, in the last few years I've killed two villains. The first was in New York – a Japanese cipher expert cracking our codes on the thirty-sixth floor of the RCA building in the Rockefeller centre, where the Japs had their consulate. I took a room on the fortieth floor of the next-door skyscraper and I could look across the street into his room and see him working. Then I got a colleague from our organization in New York and a couple of Remington thirty-thirty's with telescopic sights and silencers. We smuggled them up to my room and sat for days waiting for our chance. He shot at the man a second before me. His job was only to blast a hole through the windows so that I could shoot the Jap through it. They have tough windows at the Rocke-feller centre to keep the noise out. It worked very well. As I expected, his bullet got deflected by the glass and went God knows where. But I shot immediately after him, through the hole he had made. I got the Jap in the mouth as he turned to gape at the broken win-dow.'

Bond smoked for a minute.

'It was a pretty sound job. Nice and clean too. Three hundred yards away. No personal contact. The next time in Stockholm wasn't so pretty. I had to kill a Norwegian who was doubling against us for the Germans. He'd managed to get two of our men captured – probably bumped off for all I know. For various reasons it had to be an absolutely silent job. I chose the bedroom of his flat and a knife. And, well, he just didn't die very quickly.

'For those two jobs I was awarded a Double O number in the Service. Felt pretty clever and got a reputation for being good and tough. A Double O number in our Service means you've had to kill a chap in cold blood in the course of some job.

'Now,' he looked up again at Mathis, 'that's all very fine. The hero kills two villains, but when the hero Le Chiffre starts to kill the villain Bond and the villain Bond knows he isn't a villain at all, you see the other side of the medal. The villains and heroes get all mixed up.

'Of course,' he added, as Mathis started to expostulate, 'patriotism comes along and makes it seem fairly all right, but this country-right-or-wrong business is getting a little out-of-date. Today we are fighting Communism. Okay. If I'd been alive fifty years ago, the brand of Conservatism we have today would have been damn near called Communism and we should have been told to go and fight that. History is moving pretty quickly these days and the heroes and villains keep on changing parts.'

Mathis stared at him aghast. Then he tapped his head and put a calming hand on Bond's arm.

'You mean to say that this precious Le Chiffre who did his best to turn you into a eunuch doesn't qualify as a villain?' he asked. 'Anyone would think from the rot you talk that he had been battering your head instead of your . . .' He gestured down the bed. 'You wait till M tells you to get after another Le Chiffre. I bet you'll go after him all right. And what about SMERSH? I can tell you I don't like the idea of these chaps running around France killing anyone they feel has been a traitor to their precious political system. You're a bloody anarchist.'

He threw his arms in the air and let them fall helplessly to his sides.

Bond laughed.

'All right,' he said. 'Take our friend Le Chiffre. It's simple enough to say he was an evil man, at least it's simple enough for me because he did evil things to me. If he was here now, I wouldn't hesitate to kill him, but out of personal revenge and not, I'm afraid, for some high moral reason or for the sake of my country.'

He looked up at Mathis to see how bored he was getting with these introspective refinements of what, to Mathis, was a simple question of duty.

Mathis smiled back at him.

'Continue, my dear friend. It is interesting for me to

see this new Bond. Englishmen are so odd. They are like a nest of Chinese boxes. It takes a very long time to get to the centre of them. When one gets there the result is unrewarding, but the process is instructive and entertaining. Continue. Develop your arguments. There may be something I can use to my own chief the next time I want to get out of an unpleasant job.' He grinned maliciously.

Bond ignored him.

'Now in order to tell the difference between good and evil, we have manufactured two images representing the extremes – representing the deepest black and the purest white – and we call them God and the Devil. But in doing so we have cheated a bit. God is a clear image, you can see every hair on His beard. But the Devil. What does he look like?' Bond looked triumphantly at Mathis.

Mathis laughed ironically.

'A woman.'

'It's all very fine,' said Bond, 'but I've been thinking about these things and I'm wondering whose side I ought to be on. I'm getting very sorry for the Devil and his disciples such as the good Le Chiffre. The Devil has a rotten time and I always like to be on the side of the underdog. We don't give the poor chap a chance. There's a Good Book about goodness and how to be good and so forth, but there's no Evil Book about evil and how to be bad. The Devil has no prophets to write his Ten Commandments and no team of authors to write his biography. His case has gone completely by default. We know nothing about him but a lot of fairy stories from our parents and schoolmasters. He has no book from which we can learn the nature of evil in all its forms, with parables about evil people, proverbs about evil people, folk-lore about evil people. All we have is the living example of the people who are least good, or our own intuition.

'So,' continued Bond, warming to his argument, 'Le Chiffre was serving a wonderful purpose, a really vital purpose, perhaps the best and highest purpose of all. By his evil existence, which foolishly I have helped to destroy, he was creating a norm of badness by which, and by which alone, an opposite norm of goodness could exist. We were privileged, in our short knowledge of him, to see and estimate his wickedness and we emerge from the acquaintanceship better and more virtuous men.'

'Bravo,' said Mathis. 'I'm proud of you. You ought to be tortured every day. I really must remember to do something evil this evening. I must start at once. I have a few marks in my favour – only small ones, alas,' he added ruefully – 'but I shall work fast now that I have seen the light. What a splendid time I'm going to have. Now, let's see, where shall I start, murder, arson, rape? But no, these are peccadilloes. I must really consult the good Marquis de Sade. I am a child, an absolute child in these matters.'

His face fell.

'Ah, but our conscience, my dear Bond. What shall we do with him while we are committing some juicy sin? That is a problem. He is a crafty person this conscience and very old, as old as the first family of apes which gave birth to him. We must give that problem really careful thought or we shall spoil our enjoyment. Of course, we should murder him first, but he is a tough bird. It will be difficult, but if we succeed, we could be worse even than Le Chiffre.

'For you, dear James, it is easy. You can start off by resigning. That was a brilliant thought of yours, a splendid start to your new career. And so simple. Everyone has the revolver of resignation in his pocket. All you've got to do is pull the trigger and you will have made a big hole in your country and your conscience at the same time. A murder and a suicide with one bullet! Splendid! What a difficult and glorious profession. As for me, I must start embracing the new cause at once.'

He looked at his watch.

'Good. I've started already. I'm half an hour late for a meeting with the chief of police.'

He rose to his feet laughing.

'That was most enjoyable, my dear James. You really ought to go on the halls. Now about that little problem of yours, this business of not knowing good men from bad men and villains from heroes, and so forth. It is, of course, a difficult problem in the abstract. The secret lies in personal experience, whether you're a Chinaman or an Englishman.'

He paused at the door.

'You admit that Le Chiffre did you personal evil and that you would kill him if he appeared in front of you now?

'Well, when you get back to London you will find there are other Le Chiffres seeking to destroy you and your friends and your country. M will tell you about them. And now that you have seen a really evil man, you will know how evil they can be and you will go after them to destroy them in order to protect yourself and the people you love. You won't wait to argue about it. You know what they look like now and what they can do to people. You may be a bit more choosy about the jobs you take on. You may want to be certain that the target really is black, but there are plenty of really black targets around. There's still plenty for you to do. And you'll do it. And when you fall in love and have a mistress or a wife and children to look after, it will seem all the easier.'

Mathis opened the door and stopped on the threshold.

'Surround yourself with human beings, my dear James. They are easier to fight for than principles.'

He laughed. 'But don't let me down and become human yourself. We would lose such a wonderful machine.'

With a wave of the hand he shut the door.

'Hey,' shouted Bond.

But the footsteps went quickly off down the passage.

It was on the next day that Bond asked to see Vesper. He had not wanted to see her before. He was told that every day she came to the nursing home and asked after him. Flowers had arrived from her. Bond didn't like flowers and he told the nurse to give them to another patient. After this had happened twice, no more flowers came. Bond had not meant to offend her. He disliked having feminine things around him. Flowers seemed to ask for recognition of the person who had sent them, to be constantly transmitting a message of sympathy and affection. Bond found this irksome. He disliked being cosseted. It gave him claustrophobia.

Bond was bored at the idea of having to explain some of this to Vesper. And he was embarrassed at having to ask one or two questions which mystified him, questions about Vesper's behaviour. The answers would almost certainly make her out to be a fool. Then he had his full report to M to think about. In this he didn't want to have to criticize Vesper. It might easily cost her her job.

But above all, he admitted to himself, he shirked the answer to a more painful question.

The doctor had talked often to Bond about his injuries. He had always told him that there would be no evil effects from the terrible battering his body had received. He had said that Bond's full health would return and that none of his powers had been taken from him. But the evidence of Bond's eyes and his nerves refused these comforting assurances. He was still painfully swollen and bruised and whenever the injections wore off he was in agony. Above all, his imagination had suffered. For an hour in that room with Le Chiffre the certainty of impotence had been beaten into him and a scar had been left on his mind that could only be healed by experience.

From that day when Bond first met Vesper in the Hermitage bar, he had found her desirable and he knew that if things had been different in the night-club, if Vesper had responded in any way and if there had been no kidnapping he would have tried to sleep with her that night. Even later, in the car and outside the villa when God knows he had had other things to think about, his eroticism had been hotly aroused by the sight of her indecent nakedness.

And now when he could see her again, he was afraid. Afraid that his senses and his body would not respond to her sensual beauty. Afraid that he would feel no stir of desire and that his blood would stay cool. In his mind he had made this first meeting into a test and he was shirking the answer. That was the real reason, he admitted, why he had waited to give his body a chance to respond, why he had put off their first meeting for over a week. He would like to have put off the meeting still further, but he explained to himself that his report must be written, that any day an emissary from London would come over and want to hear the full story, that today was as good as tomorrow, that anyway he might as well know the worst.

So on the eighth day he asked for her, for the early morning when he was feeling refreshed and strong after the night's rest.

For no reason at all, he had expected that she would show some sign of her experiences, that she would look pale and even ill. He was not prepared for the tall bronzed girl in a cream tussore frock with a black belt who came happily through the door and stood smiling at him.

'Good heavens, Vesper,' he said with a wry gesture of welcome, 'you look absolutely splendid. You must thrive on disaster. How have you managed to get such a wonderful sunburn?'

'I feel very guilty,' she said sitting down beside him. 'But I've been bathing every day while you've been lying here. The doctor said I was to and Head of S said I was to, so, well, I just thought it wouldn't help you for me to be moping away all day long in my room. I've found a wonderful stretch of sand down the coast and I take my lunch and go there every day with a book and I don't come back till the evening. There's a bus that takes me there and back with only a short walk over the dunes, and I've managed to get over the fact that it's on the way down that road to the villa.'

Her voice faltered.

The mention of the villa had made Bond's eyes flicker.

She continued bravely, refusing to be defeated by Bond's lack of response.

'The doctor says it won't be long before you're allowed up. I thought perhaps . . . I thought perhaps I could take you down to this beach later on. The doctor says that bathing would be very good for you.'

Bond grunted.

'God knows when I'll be able to bathe,' he said. 'The doctor's talking through his hat. And when I can bathe it would probably be better for me to bathe alone for a bit. I don't want to frighten anybody. Apart from anything else,' he glanced pointedly down the bed, 'my body's a mass of scars and bruises. But you enjoy yourself. There's no reason why you shouldn't enjoy yourself.'

Vesper was stung by the bitterness and injustice in his voice.

'I'm sorry,' she said, 'I just thought . . . I was just trying . . .'

Suddenly her eyes filled with tears. She swallowed.

'I wanted . . . I wanted to help you get well.'

Her voice strangled. She looked piteously at him, facing the accusation in his eyes and in his manner.

Then she broke down and buried her face in her hands and sobbed.

'I'm sorry,' she said in a muffled voice. 'I'm really sorry.' With one hand she searched for a handkerchief in her bag. 'It's all my fault,' she dabbed at her eyes. 'I know it's all my fault.'

Bond at once relented. He put out a bandaged hand and laid it on her knee.

'It's all right, Vesper. I'm sorry I was so rough. It's just that I was jealous of you in the sunshine while I'm stuck here. Directly I'm well enough I'll come with you and you must show me your beach. Of course it's just what I want. It'll be wonderful to get out again.'

She pressed his hand and stood up and walked over to the window. After a moment she busied herself with her make-up. Then she came back to the bed.

Bond looked at her tenderly. Like all harsh, cold men, he was easily tipped over into sentiment. She was very beautiful and he felt warm towards her. He decided to make his questions as easy as possible.

He gave her a cigarette and for a time they talked of the visit of Head of S and of the reactions in London to the rout of Le Chiffre.

From what she said it was clear that the final object of the plan had been more than fulfilled. The story was still being splashed all over the world and correspondents of most of the English and American papers had been at Royale trying to trace the Jamaican millionaire who had defeated Le Chiffre at the tables. They had got on to Vesper, but she had covered up well. Her story was that Bond had told her he was going on to Cannes and Monte Carlo to gamble with his winnings. The hunt had moved down to the South of France. Mathis and the police had obliterated all other traces and the papers were forced to concentrate on the Strasbourg angles and the chaos in the ranks of the French Communists.

'By the way, Vesper,' said Bond after a time. 'What really happened to you after you left me in the night club? All I saw was the actual kidnapping.' He told her briefly of the scene outside the Casino.

'I'm afraid I must have lost my head,' said Vesper, avoiding Bond's eyes. 'When I couldn't see Mathis anywhere in the entrance hall I went outside and the commissionaire asked me if I was Miss Lynd, and then told me the man who had sent in the note was waiting in a car down on the right of the steps. Somehow I wasn't particularly surprised. I'd only known Mathis for a day or two and I didn't know how he worked, so I just walked down towards the car. It was away on the right and more or less in the shadows. Just as I was coming up to it, Le Chiffre's two men jumped out from behind one of the other cars in the row and simply scooped my skirt over my head.'

Vesper blushed.

'It sounds a childish trick,' she looked penitently at Bond, 'but it's really frightfully effective. One's a complete prisoner and although I screamed I don't expect any sound came out from under my skirt. I kicked out as hard as I could, but that was no use as I couldn't see and my arms were absolutely helpless. I was just a trussed chicken.

'They picked me up between them and shoved me into the back of the car. I went on struggling, of course, and when the car started and while they were trying to tie a rope or something round the top of my skirt over my head, I managed to get an arm free and throw my bag through the window. I hope it was some use.'

Bond nodded.

'It was rather instinctive. I just thought you'd have no idea what had happened to me and I was terrified. I did the first thing I could think of.'

Bond knew that it was him they had been after and that if Vesper hadn't thrown her bag out, they would probably have thrown it out themselves directly they saw him appear on the steps.

'It certainly helped,' said Bond, 'but why didn't you make any sign when they finally got me after the car smash, when I spoke to you? I was dreadfully worried. I thought they might have knocked you out or something.'

'I'm afraid I must have been unconscious,' said Vesper. 'I fainted once from lack of air and when I came to they had cut a hole in front of my face. I must have fainted again. I don't remember much until we got to the villa. I really only gathered you had been captured when I heard you try and come after me in the passage.'

'And they didn't touch you?' asked Bond. 'They didn't try and mess about with you while I was being beaten up?'

'No,' said Vesper. 'They just left me in an arm-chair. They drank and played cards – "belotte" I think it was from what I heard – and then they went to sleep. I suppose that was how SMERSH got them. They bound my legs and put me on a chair in a corner facing the wall and I saw nothing of SMERSH. I heard some odd noises. I expect they woke me up. And then what sounded like one of them falling off his chair. Then there were some soft footsteps and a door closed and then nothing happened until Mathis and the police burst in hours later. I slept most of the time. I had no idea what had happened to you, but,' she faltered, 'I did once hear a terrible scream. It sounded very far away. At least, I think it must have been a scream. At the time I thought it might have been a nightmare.'

'I'm afraid that must have been me,' said Bond.

Vesper put out a hand and touched one of his. Her eyes filled with tears.

'It's horrible,' she said. 'The things they did to you. And it was all my fault. If only . . .'

She buried her face in her hands.

'That's all right,' said Bond comfortingly. 'It's no good crying over spilt milk. It's all over now and thank heavens they let you alone.' He patted her knee. 'They were going to start on you when they'd got me really softened up,' (softened up is good, he thought to himself). 'We've got a lot to thank SMERSH for. Now, come on, let's forget about it. It certainly wasn't anything to do with you. Anybody could have fallen for that note. Anyway, it's all water over the dam,' he added cheerfully.

Vesper looked at him gratefully through her tears. 'You really promise?' she asked. 'I thought you would never forgive me. I . . . I'll try and make it up to you. Somehow.' She looked at him.

Somehow? thought Bond to himself. He looked at her. She was smiling at him. He smiled back.

'You'd better look out,' he said. 'I may hold you to that.'

She looked into his eyes and said nothing, but the enigmatic challenge was back. She pressed his hand and rose. 'A promise is a promise,' she said.

This time they both knew what the promise was.

She picked up her bag from the bed and walked to the door.

'Shall I come tomorrow?' She looked at Bond gravely.

'Yes, please, Vesper,' said Bond. 'I'd like that. Please do some more exploring. It will be fun to think of what we can do when I get up. Will you think of some things?'

'Yes,' said Vesper. 'Please get well quickly.'

They gazed at each other for a second. Then she went out and closed the door and Bond listened until the sound of her footsteps had disappeared.

From that day Bond's recovery was rapid.

He sat up in bed and wrote his report to M. He made light of what he still considered amateurish behaviour on the part of Vesper. By juggling with the emphasis, he made the kidnapping sound much more Machiavellian than it had been. He praised Vesper's coolness and composure throughout the whole episode without saying that he had found some of her actions unaccountable.

Every day Vesper came to see him and he looked forward to these visits with excitement. She talked happily of her adventures of the day before, her explorations down the coast and the restaurants where she had eaten. She had made friends with the chief of police and with one of the directors of the Casino and it was they who took her out in the evening and occasionally lent her a car during the day. She kept an eye on the repairs to the Bentley which had been towed down to coachbuilders at Rouen, and she even arranged for some new clothes to be sent out from Bond's London flat. Nothing survived from his original wardrobe. Every stitch had been cut to ribbons in the search for the forty million francs.

The Le Chiffre affair was never mentioned between them. She occasionally told Bond amusing stories of Head of S's office. She had apparently transferred there from the WRNS. And he told her of some of his adventures in the Service.

He found he could speak to her easily and he was surprised.

With most women his manner was a mixture of taciturnity and passion. The lengthy approaches to a seduction bored him almost as much as the subsequent mess of disentanglement. He found something grisly in the inevitability of the pattern of each affair. The conventional parabola – sentiment, the touch of the hand, the kiss, the passionate kiss, the feel of the body, the climax in the bed, then more bed, then less bed, then the boredom, the tears and the final bitterness – was to him shameful and hypocritical. Even more he shunned the *mise en scène* for each of these acts in the play – the meeting at a party, the restaurant, the taxi, his flat, her flat, then the week-end by the sea, then the flats again, then the furtive alibis and the final angry farewell on some doorstep in the rain.

But with Vesper there could be none of this.

In the dull room and the boredom of his treatment her presence was each day an oasis of pleasure, something to look forward to. In their talk there was nothing but companionship with a distant undertone of passion. In the background there was the unspoken zest of the promise which, in due course and in their own time, would be met. Over all there brooded the shadow of his injuries and the tantalus of their slow healing.

Whether Bond liked it or not, the branch had already escaped his knife and was ready to burst into flower.

With enjoyable steps Bond recovered. He was allowed up. Then he was allowed to sit in the garden. Then he could go for a short walk, then for a long drive. And then the afternoon came when the doctor appeared on a flying visit from Paris and pronounced him well again. His clothes were brought round by Vesper, farewells were exchanged with the nurses, and a hired car drove them away.

It was three weeks from the day when he had been on the edge of death, and now it was July and the hot summer shimmered down the coast and out to sea. Bond clasped the moment to him.

Their destination was to be a surprise for him. He had not wanted to go back to one of the big hotels in Royale and Vesper said she would find somewhere away from the town. But she insisted on being mysterious about it and only said that she had found a place he would like. He was happy to be in her hands, but he covered up his surrender by referring to their destination as 'Trou sur Mer' (she admitted it was by the sea), and lauding the rustic delights of outside lavatories, bed-bugs, and cockroaches.

Their drive was spoiled by a curious incident.

While they followed the coast road in the direction

of Les Noctambules, Bond described to her his wild chase in the Bentley, finally pointing out the curve he had taken before the crash and the exact place where the vicious carpet of spikes had been laid. He slowed the car down and leant out to show her the deep cuts in the tarmac made by the rims of the wheels and the broken branches in the hedge and the patch of oil where the car had come to rest.

But all the time she was distrait and fidgety and commented only in monosyllables. Once or twice he caught her glancing in the driving-mirror, but when he had a chance to look back through the rear window, they had just rounded a bend and he could see nothing.

Finally he took her hand.

'Something's on your mind, Vesper,' he said.

She gave him a taut, bright smile. 'It's nothing. Absolutely nothing. I had a silly idea we were being followed. It's just nerves, I suppose. This road is full of ghosts.'

Under cover of a short laugh she looked back again.

'Look.' There was an edge of panic in her voice.

Obediently Bond turned his head. Sure enough, a quarter of a mile away, a black saloon was coming after them at a good pace.

Bond laughed.

'We can't be the only people using this road,' he said. 'Anyway, who wants to follow us? We've done nothing wrong.' He patted her hand. 'It's a middle-aged commercial traveller in car-polish on his way to Le Havre.

He's probably thinking of his lunch and his mistress in Paris. Really, Vesper, you mustn't think evil of the innocent.'

'I expect you're right,' she said nervously. 'Anyway, we're nearly there.'

She relapsed into silence and gazed out of the window.

Bond could still feel her tenseness. He smiled to himself at what he took to be simply a hangover from their recent adventures. But he decided to humour her and when they came to a small lane leading towards the sea and slowed to turn down it, he told the driver to stop directly they were off the main road.

Hidden by the tall hedge, they watched together through the rear window.

Through the quiet hum of summer noises they could hear the car approaching. Vesper dug her fingers into his arm. The pace of the car did not alter as it approached their hiding-place and they had only a brief glimpse of a man's profile as a black saloon tore by.

It was true that he seemed to glance quickly towards them, but above them in the hedge there was a gaily painted sign pointing down the lane and announcing '*L'Auberge du Fruit Défendu, crustaces, fritures*'. It was obvious to Bond that it was this that had caught the driver's eye.

As the rattle of the car's exhaust diminished down the road, Vesper sank back into her corner. Her face was pale.

'He looked at us,' she said, 'I told you so. I knew we were being followed. Now they know where we are.'

Bond could not contain his impatience. 'Bunkum,' he said. 'He was looking at that sign.' He pointed it out to Vesper.

She looked slightly relieved. 'Do you really think so?' she asked. 'Yes. I see. Of course, you must be right. Come on. I'm sorry to be so stupid. I don't know what came over me.'

She leant forward and talked to the driver through the partition, and the car moved on. She sank back and turned a bright face towards Bond. The colour had almost come back to her cheeks. 'I really am sorry. It's just that . . . it's that I can't believe everything's over and there's no one to be frightened of any more.' She pressed his hand. 'You must think me very stupid.'

'Of course not,' said Bond. 'But really nobody could be interested in us now. Forget it all. The whole job's finished, wiped up. This is our holiday and there's not a cloud in the sky. Is there?' he persisted.

'No, of course not.' She shook herself slightly. 'I'm mad. Now we'll be there in a second. I do hope you're going to like it.'

They both leant forward. Animation was back in her face and the incident left only the smallest question-mark hanging in the air. Even that faded as they came through the dunes and saw the sea and the modest little inn amongst the pines.

'It's not very grand, I'm afraid,' said Vesper. 'But it's

very clean and the food's wonderful.' She looked at him anxiously.

She need not have worried. Bond loved the place at first sight – the terrace leading almost to the high-tide mark, the low two-storied house with gay brick-red awnings over the windows and the crescent-shaped bay of blue water and golden sands. How many times in his life would he have given anything to have turned off a main road to find a lost corner like this where he could let the world go by and live in the sea from dawn to dusk? And now he was to have a whole week of this. And of Vesper. In his mind he fingered the necklace of the days to come.

They drew up in the courtyard behind the house and the proprietor and his wife came out to greet them.

Monsieur Versoix was a middle-aged man with one arm. The other he had lost fighting with the Free French in Madagascar. He was a friend of the chief of police of Royale and it was the Commissaire who had suggested the place to Vesper and had spoken to the proprietor on the telephone. As a result, nothing was going to be too good for them.

Madame Versoix had been interrupted in the middle of preparing dinner. She wore an apron and held a wooden spoon in one hand. She was younger than her husband, chubby and handsome and warm-eyed. Instinctively Bond guessed that they had no children and that they gave their thwarted affection to their friends and some regular customers, and probably to some pets. He thought that their life was probably something of a struggle and that the inn must be very lonely in winter-time with the big seas and the noise of the wind in the pines.

The proprietor showed them to their rooms.

Vesper's was a double room and Bond was next door, at the corner of the house, with one window looking out to sea and another with a view of the distant arm of the bay. There was a bathroom between them. Everything was spotless, and sparsely comfortable.

The proprietor was pleased when they both showed their delight. He said that dinner would be at seven-thirty and that *Madame la patronne* was preparing broiled lobsters with melted butter. He was sorry that they were so quiet just then. It was Tuesday. There would be more people at the week-end. The season had not been good. Generally they had plenty of English people staying, but times were difficult over there and the English just came for a week-end at Royale and then went home after losing their money at the Casino. It was not like the old days. He shrugged his shoulders philosophically. But then no day was like the day before, and no century like the previous one, and . . .

'Quite so,' said Bond.

They were talking on the threshold of Vesper's room. When the proprietor left them, Bond pushed her inside and closed the door. Then he put his hands on her shoulders and kissed her on both cheeks.

'This is heaven,' he said.

Then he saw that her eyes were shining. Her hands came up and rested on his forearms. He stepped right up against her and his arms dropped round her waist. Her head went back and her mouth opened beneath his.

'My darling,' he said. He plunged his mouth down on to hers, forcing her teeth apart with his tongue and feeling her own tongue working at first shyly then more passionately. He slipped his hands down to her swelling buttocks and gripped them fiercely, pressing the centres of their bodies together. Panting, she slipped her mouth away from his and they clung together while he rubbed his cheek against hers and felt her hard breasts pressing into him. Then he reached up and seized her hair and bent her head back until he could kiss her again. She pushed him away and sank back exhausted on to the bed. For a moment they looked at each other hungrily.

'I'm sorry, Vesper,' he said. 'I didn't mean to then.'

She shook her head, dumb with the storm which had passed through her.

He came and sat beside her and they looked at each other with lingering tenderness as the tide of passion ebbed in their veins.

She leant over and kissed him on the corner of the mouth, then she brushed the black comma of hair back from his damp forehead.

'My darling,' she said. 'Give me a cigarette. I don't know where my bag is.' She looked vaguely round the room.

Bond lit one for her and put it between her lips. She took a deep lungful of smoke and let it pour out through her mouth with a slow sigh.

Bond put his arm round her, but she got up and walked over to the window. She stood there with her back to him.

Bond looked down at his hands and saw they were still trembling.

'It's going to take some time to get ready for dinner,' said Vesper still not looking at him. 'Why don't you go and bathe? I'll unpack for you.'

Bond left the bed and came and stood close against her. He put his arms round her and put a hand over each breast. They filled his hands and the nipples were hard against his fingers. She put her hands over his and pressed them into her, but still she looked away from him out of the window.

'Not now,' she said in a low voice.

Bond bent and burrowed his lips into the nape of her neck. For a moment he strained her hard to him, then he let her go.

'All right, Vesper,' he said.

He walked over to the door and looked back. She had not moved. For some reason he thought she was crying. He took a step towards her and then realized that there was nothing to say between them then.

'My love,' he said.

Then he went out and shut the door.

Bond walked along to his room and sat down on the bed.

He felt weak from the passion which had swept through his body. He was torn between the desire to fall back full-length on the bed and his longing to be cooled and revived by the sea. He played with the choice for a moment, then he went over to his suitcase and took out white linen bathing-drawers and a dark blue pyjama-suit.

Bond had always disliked pyjamas and had slept naked until in Hong Kong at the end of the war he came across the perfect compromise. This was a pyjama-coat which came almost down to the knees. It had no buttons, but there was a loose belt round the waist. The sleeves were wide and short, ending just above the elbow. The result was cool and comfortable and now when he slipped the coat on over his trunks, all his bruises and scars were hidden except the thin white bracelets on wrists and ankles and the mark of SMERSH on his right hand.

He slipped his feet into a pair of dark-blue leather sandals and went downstairs and out of the house and across the terrace to the beach. As he passed across the front of the house he thought of Vesper, but he refrained from looking up to see if she was still standing at the window. If she saw him, she gave no sign.

He walked along the waterline on the hard golden sand until he was out of sight of the inn. Then he threw off his pyjama-coat and took a short run and a quick flat dive into the small waves. The beach shelved quickly and he kept underwater as long as he could, swimming with powerful strokes and feeling the soft coolness all over him. Then he surfaced and brushed the hair out of his eyes. It was nearly seven and the sun had lost much of its heat. Before long it would sink beneath the further arm of the bay, but now it was straight in his eyes and he turned on his back and swam away from it so that he could keep it with him as long as possible.

When he came ashore nearly a mile down the bay the shadows had already engulfed his distant pyjamas but he knew he had time to lie on the hard sand and dry before the tide of dusk reached him.

He took off his bathing-trunks and looked down at his body. There were only a few traces left of his injuries. He shrugged his shoulders and lay down with his limbs spread out in a star and gazed up at the empty blue sky and thought of Vesper.

His feelings for her were confused and he was impatient with the confusion. They had been so simple. He had intended to sleep with her as soon as he could, because he desired her and also because, and he admitted it to himself, he wanted coldly to put the repairs to his body to the final test. He thought they would sleep together for a few days and then he might see something of her in London. Then would come the inevitable disengagement which would be all the easier because of their positions in the Service. If it was not easy, he could go off on an assignment abroad or, which was also in his mind, he could resign and travel to different parts of the world as he had always wanted.

But somehow she had crept under his skin and over the last two weeks his feelings had gradually changed.

He found her companionship easy and unexacting. There was something enigmatic about her which was a constant stimulus. She gave little of her real personality away and he felt that however long they were together there would always be a private room inside her which he could never invade. She was thoughtful and full of consideration without being slavish and without compromising her arrogant spirit. And now he knew that she was profoundly, excitingly sensual, but that the conquest of her body, because of the central privacy in her, would each time have the sweet tang of rape. Loving her physically would each time be a thrilling voyage without the anticlimax of arrival. She would surrender herself avidly, he thought, and greedily enjoy all the intimacies of the bed without ever allowing herself to be possessed.

Naked, Bond lay and tried to push away the conclusions he read in the sky. He turned his head and looked down the beach and saw that the shadows of the headland were almost reaching for him.

He stood up and brushed off as much of the sand as he could reach. He reflected that he would have a bath when he got in and he absent-mindedly picked up his trunks and started walking back along the beach. It was only when he reached his pyjama-coat and bent to pick it up that he realized he was still naked. Without bothering about the trunks, he slipped on the light coat and walked on to the hotel.

At that moment his mind was made up.

When he got back to his room he was touched to find all his belongings put away and in the bathroom his toothbrush and shaving things neatly arranged at one end of the glass shelf over the wash-basin. At the other end was Vesper's toothbrush and one or two small bottles and a jar of face-cream.

He glanced at the bottles and was surprised to see that one contained nembutal sleeping-pills. Perhaps her nerves had been more shaken by the events at the villa than he had imagined.

The bath had been filled for him and there was a new flask of some expensive pine bath-essence on a chair beside it with his towel.

'Vesper,' he called.

'Yes?'

'You really are the limit. You make me feel like an expensive gigolo.'

'I was told to look after you. I'm only doing what I was told.'

'Darling, the bath's absolutely right. Will you marry me?'

She snorted. 'You need a slave, not a wife.'

'I want you.'

'Well, I want my lobster and champagne, so hurry up.'

'All right, all right,' said Bond.

He dried himself and dressed in a white shirt and dark blue slacks. He hoped that she would be dressed as simply and he was pleased when, without knocking, she appeared in the doorway wearing a blue linen shirt which had faded to the colour of her eyes and a dark red skirt in pleated cotton.

'I couldn't wait. I was famished. My room's over the kitchen and I've been tortured by the wonderful smells.'

He came over and put his arm round her.

She took his hand and together they went downstairs out on to the terrace where their table had been laid in the light cast by the empty dining-room.

The champagne which Bond had ordered on their arrival stood on a plated wine-cooler beside their table and Bond poured out two full glasses. Vesper busied herself with a delicious home-made liver *paté* and helped them both to the crisp French bread and the thick square of deep yellow butter set in chips of ice.

They looked at each other and drank deeply and Bond filled their glasses again to the rim.

While they ate Bond told her of his bathe and they talked of what they would do in the morning. All through the meal they left unspoken their feelings for each other, but in Vesper's eyes as much as in Bond's there was excited anticipation of the night. They let their hands and their feet touch from time to time as if to ease the tension in their bodies.

When the lobster had come and gone and the second bottle of champagne was half-empty and they had just ladled thick cream over their *fraises des bois*, Vesper gave a deep sigh of contentment.

'I'm behaving like a pig,' she said happily. 'You always give me all the things I like best. I've never been so spoiled before.' She gazed across the terrace at the moonlit bay. 'I wish I deserved it.' Her voice had a wry undertone.

'What do you mean?' asked Bond surprised.

'Oh, I don't know. I suppose people get what they deserve, so perhaps I do deserve it.'

She looked at him and smiled. Her eyes narrowed quizzically.

'You really don't know much about me,' she said suddenly.

Bond was surprised by the undertone of seriousness in her voice.

'Quite enough,' he said laughing. 'All I need until tomorrow and the next day and the next. You don't know much about me for the matter of that.' He poured out more champagne.

Vesper looked at him thoughtfully.

'People are islands,' she said. 'They don't really touch. However close they are, they're really quite separate. Even if they've been married for fifty years.'

Bond thought with dismay that she must be going into a *vin triste*. Too much champagne had made her melancholy. But suddenly she gave a happy laugh. 'Don't look so worried.' She leaned forward and put her hand over his. 'I was only being sentimental. Anyway, my island feels very close to your island tonight.' She took a sip of champagne.

Bond laughed, relieved. 'Let's join up and make a peninsula,' he said. 'Now, directly we've finished the strawberries.'

'No,' she said, flirting. 'I must have coffee.'

'And brandy,' countered Bond.

The small shadow had passed. The second small shadow. This too left a tiny question-mark hanging in the air. It quickly dissolved as warmth and intimacy enclosed them again.

When they had had their coffee and Bond was sipping his brandy, Vesper picked up her bag and came and stood behind him.

'I'm tired,' she said, resting a hand on his shoulder.

He reached up and held it there and they stayed motionless for a moment. She bent down and lightly brushed his hair with her lips. Then she was gone and a few seconds later the light came on in her room.

Bond smoked and waited until it had gone out. Then he followed her, pausing only to say good night to the proprietor and his wife and thank them for the dinner. They exchanged compliments and he went upstairs.

It was only half past nine when he stepped into her

room from the bathroom and closed the door behind him.

The moonlight shone through the half-closed shutters and lapped at the secret shadows in the snow of her body on the broad bed.

Bond awoke in his own room at dawn and for a time he lay and stroked his memories.

Then he got quietly out of bed and in his pyjamacoat he crept past Vesper's door and out of the house to the beach.

The sea was smooth and quiet in the sunrise. The small pink waves idly licked the sand. It was cold, but he took off his jacket and wandered naked along the edge of the sea to the point where he had bathed the evening before, then he walked slowly and deliberately into the water until it was just below his chin. He took his feet off the bottom and sank, holding his nose with one hand and shutting his eyes, feeling the cold water comb his body and his hair.

The mirror of the bay was unbroken except where it seemed a fish had jumped. Under the water he imagined the tranquil scene and wished that Vesper could just then come through the pines and be astonished to see him suddenly erupt from the empty seascape.

When after a full minute he came to the surface in a froth of spray, he was disappointed. There was no one in sight. For a time he swam and drifted and then when the sun seemed hot enough, he came in to the beach and lay on his back and revelled in the body which the night had given back to him.

As on the evening before, he stared up into the empty sky and saw the same answer there.

After a while he rose and walked back slowly along the beach to his pyjama-coat.

That day he would ask Vesper to marry him. He was quite certain. It was only a question of choosing the right moment.

As he walked quietly from the terrace into the half-darkness of the still shuttered dining-room, he was surprised to see Vesper emerge from the glass-fronted telephone booth near the front door and softly turn up the stairs towards their rooms.

'Vesper,' he called, thinking she must have had some urgent message which might concern them both.

She turned quickly, a hand up to her mouth.

For a moment longer than necessary she stared at him, her eyes wide.

'What is it, darling?' he asked, vaguely troubled and fearing some crisis in their lives.

'Oh,' she said breathlessly, 'you made me jump. It was only . . . I was just telephoning to Mathis. To Mathis,' she repeated. 'I wondered if he could get me another frock. You know, from that girl-friend I told you about. The *vendeuse*. You see,' she talked quickly, her words coming out in a persuasive jumble, 'I've really got nothing to wear. I thought I'd catch him at home before he went to the office. I don't know my friend's telephone number and I thought it would be a surprise for you. I didn't want you to hear me moving and wake you up. Is the water nice? Have you bathed? You ought to have waited for me.'

'It's wonderful,' said Bond, deciding to relieve her mind, though irritated with her obvious guilt over this childish mystery. 'You must go in and we'll have breakfast on the terrace. I'm ravenous. I'm sorry I made you jump. I was just startled to see anyone about at this hour of the morning.'

He put his arm round her, but she disengaged herself, and moved quickly on up the stairs.

'It was such a surprise to see you,' she said, trying to cover the incident up with a light touch. 'You looked like a ghost, a drowned man, with the hair down over your eyes like that.' She laughed harshly. Hearing the harshness, she turned the laugh into a cough.

'I hope I haven't caught cold,' she said.

She kept on patching up the edifice of her deceit until Bond wanted to spank her and tell her to relax and tell the truth. Instead he just gave her a reassuring pat on the back outside her room and told her to hurry up and have her bathe.

Then he went on to his room.

That was the end of the integrity of their love. The succeeding days were a shambles of falseness and hypocrisy, mingled with her tears and moments of animal passion to which she abandoned herself with a greed made indecent by the hollowness of their days.

Several times Bond tried to break down the dreadful

walls of mistrust. Again and again he brought up the subject of the telephone call, but she obstinately bolstered up her story with embellishments which Bond knew she had thought out afterwards. She even accused Bond of thinking she had another lover.

These scenes always ended in her bitter tears and in moments almost of hysteria.

Each day the atmosphere became more hateful.

It seemed fantastic to Bond that human relationships could collapse into dust overnight and he searched his mind again and again for a reason.

He felt that Vesper was just as horrified as he was and, if anything, her misery seemed greater than his. But the mystery of the telephone conversation which Vesper angrily, almost fearfully it seemed to Bond, refused to explain was a shadow which grew darker with other small mysteries and reticences.

Already at luncheon on that day things got worse.

After a breakfast which was an effort for both of them, Vesper said she had a headache and would stay in her room out of the sun. Bond took a book and walked for miles down the beach. By the time he returned he had argued to himself that they would be able to sort the problem out over lunch.

Directly they sat down, he apologized gaily for having startled her at the telephone booth and then he dismissed the subject and went on to describe what he had seen on his walk. But Vesper was distrait and commented only in monosyllables. She toyed with her food and she avoided Bond's eyes and gazed past him with an air of preoccupation.

When she had failed once or twice to respond to some conversational gambit or other, Bond also relapsed into silence and occupied himself with his own gloomy thoughts.

All of a sudden she stiffened. Her fork fell with a clatter on to the edge of her plate and then noisily off the table on to the terrace.

Bond looked up. She had gone as white as a sheet and she was looking over his shoulder with terror in her face.

Bond turned his head and saw that a man had just taken his place at a table on the opposite side of the terrace, well away from them. He seemed ordinary enough, perhaps rather sombrely dressed, but in his first quick glance Bond put him down as some business-man on his way along the coast who had just happened on the inn or had picked it out of the Michelin.

'What is it, darling?' he asked anxiously.

Vesper's eyes never moved from the distant figure.

'It's the man in the car,' she said in a stifled voice. 'The man who was following us. I know it is.'

Bond looked again over his shoulder. The *patron* was discussing the menu with the new customer. It was a perfectly normal scene. They exchanged smiles over some item on the menu and apparently agreed that it would suit for the *patron* took the card and with, Bond guessed, a final exchange about the wine, he withdrew.

The man seemed to realize that he was being watched. He looked up and gazed incuriously at them for a moment. Then he reached for a brief-case on the chair beside him, extracted a newspaper and started to read it, his elbows propped up on the table.

When the man had turned his face towards them, Bond noticed that he had a black patch over one eye. It was not tied with a tape across the eye, but screwed in like a monocle. Otherwise he seemed a friendly middle-aged man, with dark brown hair brushed straight back, and, as Bond had seen while he was talking to the *patron*, particularly large, white teeth.

He turned back to Vesper. 'Really, darling. He looks very innocent. Are you sure he's the same man? We can't expect to have this place entirely to ourselves.'

Vesper's face was still a white mask. She was clutching the edge of the table with both hands. He thought she was going to faint and almost rose to come round to her, but she made a gesture to stop him. Then she reached for a glass of wine and took a deep draught. The glass rattled on her teeth and she brought up her other hand to help. Then she put the glass down.

She looked at him with dull eyes.

'I know it's the same.'

He tried to reason with her, but she paid no attention. After glancing once or twice over his shoulder with eyes that held a curious submissiveness, she said that her headache was still bad and that she would spend the afternoon in her room. She left the table and walked indoors without a backward glance.

Bond was determined to set her mind at rest. He ordered coffee to be brought to the table and then he rose and walked swiftly to the courtyard. The black Peugeot which stood there might indeed have been the saloon they had seen, but it might equally have been one of a million others on the French roads. He took a quick glance inside, but the interior was empty and when he tried the boot, it was locked. He made a note of the Paris number-plate then he went quickly to the lavatory adjoining the dining-room, pulled the chain and walked out on to the terrace.

The man was eating and didn't look up.

Bond sat down in Vesper's chair so that he could watch the other table.

A few minutes later the man asked for the bill, paid it and left. Bond heard the Peugeot start up and soon the noise of its exhaust had disappeared in the direction of the road to Royale.

When the *patron* came back to his table, Bond explained that Madame had unfortunately a slight touch of sunstroke. After the *patron* had expressed his regret and enlarged on the dangers of going out of doors in almost any weather, Bond casually asked about the other customer. 'He reminds me of a friend who also lost an eye. They wear similar black patches.'

The *patron* answered that the man was a stranger. He had been pleased with his lunch and had said that he would be passing that way again in a day or two and would take another meal at the *auberge*. Apparently he was Swiss, which could also be seen from his accent. He was a traveller in watches. It was shocking to have only one eye. The strain of keeping that patch in place all day long. He supposed one got used to it.

'It is indeed very sad,' said Bond. 'You also have been unlucky,' he gestured to the proprietor's empty sleeve. 'I myself was very fortunate.'

For a time they talked about the war. Then Bond rose.

'By the way,' he said, 'Madame had an early telephone call which I must remember to pay for. Paris. An Elysée number I think,' he added, remembering that that was Mathis's exchange.

'Thank you, monsieur, but the matter is regulated. I was speaking to Royale this morning and the exchange mentioned that one of my guests had put through a call to Paris and that there had been no answer. They wanted to know if Madame would like the call kept in. I'm afraid the matter escaped my mind. Perhaps Monsieur would mention it to Madame. But, let me see, it was an Invalides number the exchange referred to.'

The next two days were much the same.

On the fourth day of their stay Vesper went off early to Royale. A taxi came and fetched her and brought her back. She said she needed some medicine.

That night she made a special effort to be gay. She drank a lot and when they went upstairs, she led him into her bedroom and made passionate love to him. Bond's body responded, but afterwards she cried bitterly into her pillow and Bond went to his room in grim despair.

He could hardly sleep and in the early hours he heard her door open softly. Some small sounds came from downstairs. He was sure she was in the telephone booth. Very soon he heard her door softly close and he guessed that again there had been no reply from Paris.

This was Saturday.

On Sunday the man with the black patch was back again. Bond knew it directly he looked up from his lunch and saw her face. He had told her all that the *patron* had told him, withholding only the man's statement that he might be back. He had thought it would worry her.

He had also telephoned Mathis in Paris and checked

on the Peugeot. It had been hired from a respectable firm two weeks before. The customer had had a Swiss triptyque. His name was Adolph Gettler. He had given a bank in Zurich as his address.

Mathis had got on to the Swiss police. Yes, the bank had an account in this name. It was little used. Herr Gettler was understood to be connected with the watch industry. Inquiries could be pursued if there was a charge against him.

Vesper had shrugged her shoulders at the information. This time when the man appeared she left her lunch in the middle and went straight up to her room.

Bond made up his mind. When he had finished, he followed her. Both her doors were locked and when he made her let him in, he saw that she had been sitting in the shadows by the window, watching, he presumed.

Her face was of cold stone. He led her to the bed and drew her down beside him. They sat stiffly, like people in a railway carriage.

'Vesper,' he said, holding her cold hands in his, 'we can't go on like this. We must finish with it. We are torturing each other and there is only one way of stopping it. Either you must tell me what all this is about or we must leave. At once.'

She said nothing and her hands were lifeless in his.

'My darling,' he said. 'Won't you tell me? Do you know, that first morning I was coming back to ask you to marry me. Can't we go back to the beginning again? What is this dreadful nightmare that is killing us?'

At first she said nothing, then a tear rolled slowly down her cheek.

'You mean you would have married me?'

Bond nodded.

'Oh my God,' she said. 'My God.' She turned and clutched him, pressing her face against his chest.

He held her closely to him. 'Tell me, my love,' he said. 'Tell me what's hurting you.'

Her sobs became quieter.

'Leave me for a little,' she said and a new note had come into her voice. A note of resignation. 'Let me think for a little.' She kissed his face and held it between her hands. She looked at him with yearning. 'Darling, I'm trying to do what's best for us. Please believe me. But it's terrible. I'm in a frightful . . .' She wept again, clutching him like a child with nightmares.

He soothed her, stroking the long black hair and kissing her softly.

'Go away now,' she said. 'I must have time to think. We've got to do something.'

She took his handkerchief and dried her eyes.

She led him to the door and there they held tightly to each other. Then he kissed her again and she shut the door behind him.

That evening most of the gayness and intimacy of their first night came back. She was excited and some of her laughter sounded brittle, but Bond was determined to fall in with her new mood and it was only at the end of dinner that he made a passing remark which made her pause.

She put her hand over his.

'Don't talk about it now,' she said. 'Forget it now. It's all past. I'll tell you about it in the morning.'

She looked at him and suddenly her eyes were full of tears. She found a handkerchief in her bag and dabbed at them.

'Give me some more champagne,' she said. She gave a queer little laugh. 'I want a lot more. You drink much more than me. It's not fair.'

They sat and drank together until the bottle was finished. Then she got to her feet. She knocked against her chair and giggled.

'I do believe I'm tight,' she said, 'how disgraceful. Please, James, don't be ashamed of me. I did so want to be gay. And I am gay.'

She stood behind him and ran her fingers through his black hair.

'Come up quickly,' she said. 'I want you badly tonight.'

She blew a kiss at him and was gone.

For two hours they made slow, sweet love in a mood of happy passion which the day before Bond would never have thought they could regain. The barriers of self-consciousness and mistrust seemed to have vanished and the words they spoke to each other were innocent and true again and there was no shadow between them.

'You must go now,' said Vesper when Bond had slept for a while in her arms.

As if to take back her words she held him more closely to her, murmuring endearments and pressing her body down the whole length of his.

When he finally rose and bent to smooth back her hair and finally kiss her eyes and her mouth good night, she reached out and turned on the light.

'Look at me,' she said, 'and let me look at you.'

He knelt beside her.

She examined every line on his face as if she was seeing him for the first time. Then she reached up and put an arm round his neck. Her deep blue eyes were swimming with tears as she drew his head slowly towards her and kissed him gently on the lips. Then she let him go and turned off the light.

'Good night, my dearest love,' she said.

Bond bent and kissed her. He tasted the tears on her cheek.

He went to the door and looked back.

'Sleep well, my darling,' he said. 'Don't worry, everything's all right now.'

He closed the door softly and walked to his room with a full heart.

The *patron* brought him the letter in the morning.

He burst into Bond's room holding the envelope in front of him as if it was on fire.

'There has been a terrible accident. Madame . . .'

Bond hurled himself out of bed and through the bathroom, but the communicating door was locked. He dashed back and through his room and down the corridor past a shrinking, terrified maid.

Vesper's door was open. The sunlight through the shutters lit up the room. Only her black hair showed above the sheet and her body under the bedclothes was straight and moulded like a stone effigy on a tomb.

Bond fell on his knees beside her and drew back the sheet.

She was asleep. She must be. Her eyes were closed. There was no change in the dear face. She was just as she would look and yet, and yet she was so still, no movement, no pulse, no breath. That was it. There was no breath.

Later the *patron* came and touched him on the shoulder. He pointed at the empty glass on the table beside her. There were white dregs in the bottom of it. It stood beside her book and her cigarettes and matches and the small pathetic litter of her mirror and lipstick and handkerchief. And on the floor the empty bottle of sleeping-pills, the pills Bond had seen in the bathroom that first evening.

Bond rose to his feet and shook himself. The *patron* was holding out the letter towards him. He took it.

'Please notify the Commissaire,' said Bond. 'I will be in my room when he wants me.'

He walked blindly away without a backward glance.

He sat on the edge of his bed and gazed out of the window at the peaceful sea. Then he stared dully at the envelope. It was addressed simply in a large round hand 'Pour Lui'.

The thought passed through Bond's mind that she must have left orders to be called early, so that it would not be he who found her.

He turned the envelope over. Not long ago it was her warm tongue which had sealed the flap.

He gave a sudden shrug and opened it.

It was not long. After the first few words he read it quickly, the breath coming harshly through his nostrils.

Then he threw it down on the bed as if it had been a scorpion.

My darling James [the letter opened],

I love you with all my heart and while you read these words I hope you still love me because, now, with these words, this is the last moment that your love will last. So good-bye, my sweet love, while we still love each other. Good-bye, my darling.

I am an agent of the MWD. Yes, I am a double agent for the Russians. I was taken on a year after the war and I have worked for them ever since. I was in love with a Pole in the RAF. Until you, I still was. You can find out who he was. He had two DSOs and after the war he was trained by M and dropped back into Poland. They caught him and by torturing him they found out a lot and also about me. They came after me and told me he could live if I would work for them. He knew nothing of this, but he was allowed to write to me. The letter arrived on the fifteenth of each month. I found I couldn't stop. I couldn't bear the idea of a fifteenth coming round without his letter. It would mean that I had killed him. I tried to give them as little as possible. You must believe me about this. Then it came to you. I told them you had been given this job at Royale, what your cover was and so on. That was why they knew about you before you arrived and why they had time to put the microphones in. They suspected Le Chiffre, but they didn't know what your assignment was except that it was something to do with him. That was all I told them.

Then I was told not to stand behind you in the Casino and to see that neither Mathis nor Leiter did. That was why the gunman was nearly able to shoot you. Then I had to stage that kidnapping. You may have wondered why I was so quiet in the night-club. They didn't hurt me because I was working for MWD.

But when I found out what had been done to you, even though it was Le Chiffre who did it and he turned out to be a traitor, I decided I couldn't go on. By that time I had begun to fall in love with you. They wanted me to find out things from you while you were recovering, but I refused. I was controlled from Paris. I had to ring up an Invalides number twice a day. They threatened me, and finally they withdrew my control and I knew my lover in Poland would have to die. But they were afraid I would talk, I suppose, and I got a final warning that SMERSH would come for me if I didn't obey them. I took no notice. I was in love with you. Then I saw the man with the black patch in the Splendide and I found he had been making inquiries about my movements. This was the day before we came down here. I hoped I could shake him off. I decided that we would have an affair and I would escape to South America from Le Havre. I hoped I would have a baby of yours and be able to start again somewhere. But they followed us. You can't get away from them.

I knew it would be the end of our love if I told you. I realized that I could either wait to be killed by SMERSH, would perhaps get you killed too, or I could kill myself.

There it is, my darling love. You can't stop me calling you that or saying that I love you. I am taking that with me and the memories of you.

I can't tell you much to help you. The Paris number was Invalides 55200. I never met any of them in London.

Everything was done through an accommodation address, a newsagent's at 450 Charing Cross Place.

At our first dinner together you talked about that man in Yugoslavia who was found guilty of treason. He said: 'I was carried away by the gale of the world.' That's my only excuse. That, and for love of the man whose life I tried to save.

It's late now and I'm tired, and you're just through two doors. But I've got to be brave. You might save my life, but I couldn't bear the look in your dear eyes.

My love, my love.

V.

Bond threw the letter down. Mechanically he brushed his fingers together. Suddenly he banged his temples with his fists and stood up. For a moment he looked out towards the quiet sea, then he cursed aloud, one harsh obscenity.

His eyes were wet and he dried them.

He pulled on a shirt and trousers and with a set cold face he walked down and shut himself in the telephone booth.

While he was getting through to London, he calmly reviewed the facts of Vesper's letter. They all fitted. The little shadows and question-marks of the past four weeks, which his instinct had noted but his mind rejected, all stood out now like signposts.

He saw her now only as a spy. Their love and his grief were relegated to the boxroom of his mind. Later, perhaps they would be dragged out, dispassionately examined, and then bitterly thrust back with other sentimental baggage he would rather forget. Now he could only think of her treachery to the Service and to her country and of the damage it had done. His professional mind was completely absorbed with the consequences – the covers which must have been blown over the years, the codes which the enemy must have broken, the secrets which must have leaked from the centre of the very section devoted to penetrating the Soviet Union.

It was ghastly. God knew how the mess would be cleared up.

He ground his teeth. Suddenly Mathis's words came back to him: 'There are plenty of really black targets around,' and, earlier, 'What about SMERSH? I don't like the idea of these chaps running around France killing anyone they feel has been a traitor to their precious political system.'

How soon Mathis had been proved right and how soon his own little sophistries had been exploded in his face!

While he, Bond, had been playing Red Indians through the years (yes, Le Chiffre's description was perfectly accurate), the real enemy had been working quietly, coldly, without heroics, right there at his elbow.

He suddenly had a vision of Vesper walking down a corridor with documents in her hand. On a tray. They just got it on a tray while the cool secret agent with a

Double O number was gallivanting round the world –
playing Red Indians.

His fingernails dug into the palms of his hands and
his body sweated with shame.

Well, it was not too late. Here was a target for him,
right to hand. He would take on SMERSH and hunt it
down. Without SMERSH, without this cold weapon of
death and revenge, the MWD would be just another
bunch of civil servant spies, no better and no worse
than any of the western services.

SMERSH was the spur. Be faithful, spy well, or you
die. Inevitably and without any question, you will be
hunted down and killed.

It was the same with the whole Russian machine.
Fear was the impulse. For them it was always safer to
advance than to retreat. Advance against the enemy
and the bullet might miss you. Retreat, evade, betray,
and the bullet would never miss.

But now he would attack the arm that held the whip
and the gun. The business of espionage could be left to
the white-collar boys. They could spy, and catch the
spies. He would go after the threat behind the spies,
the threat that made them spy.

The telephone rang and Bond snatched up the
receiver.

He was on to 'the Link', the outside liaison officer
who was the only man in London he might telephone
from abroad. Then only in dire necessity.

'This is 007 speaking. This is an open line. It's an

emergency. Can you hear me? Pass this on at once. 3030 was a double, working for Redland.

'Yes, dammit, I said "was". The bitch is dead now.'